PUFFIN BOOKS

you must be Layla

YASSMIN
ABDEL-MAGIED

you
must be
Layla

PUFFIN

PUFFIN BOOKS

UK | USA | Canada | Ireland | Australia
India | New Zealand | South Africa

Puffin Books is part of the Penguin Random House group of companies
whose addresses can be found at global.penguinrandomhouse.com.

www.penguin.co.uk
www.puffin.co.uk
www.ladybird.co.uk

First published by Penguin Random House Australia 2019
First published in Great Britain by Puffin Books 2020

001

Set in 13/20 pt Bembo Book MT Std
Typeset by Jouve (UK), Milton Keynes
Printed and bound in Great Britain by Clays Ltd, Elcograf S.p.A.

A CIP catalogue record for this book is available from the British Library

ISBN: 978–0–241–44049–0

All correspondence to:
Puffin Books
Penguin Random House Children's
80 Strand, London WC2R 0RL

To all the young girls of the diaspora

A Note

When Arabic words are written with the Roman alphabet, numerals are used to translate sounds that don't exist in English. You can find a list of the Arabic words used in the book, with their English translations, at the back of the book.

Chapter 1

'Gah, this skirt is the *worst*,' Layla muttered to herself as she studied the mirror on the back of her wooden bedroom door. Biting her lip, she tucked the cream shirt into her maroon skirt, untucked it, then tucked it back in again, weighing up which option was less ridiculous. OMG! Nothing was working. How was she supposed to make any friends at this new school when the uniform made her look like a nun? Layla squinted at her reflection, her bushy black eyebrows furrowing together. She wasn't even like one of those dope singing nuns from that movie *Sister Act 2*. No, in this uniform she looked like a mean old lady who'd realized marrying God meant there was nobody around to help do the dishes.

'*Oh, happy day* . . .' Layla started humming, distracting herself with the thought of the famous gospel tune. The thirteen-year-old loved singing, even though her older brother, Ozzie, always said she sounded like a choking chimpanzee. *He doesn't appreciate my talent!* Layla giggled to herself.

Deciding to go with the shirt tucked in, she turned her attention to the next challenge: her headscarf. It was a shiny polyester maroon piece, made to match the burgundy skirt of the school uniform. The sheer polyester was lined with a slightly darker ribbon, giving it a formal look. Layla styled it in the traditional Sudanese way: the rectangle scarf wrapped round her head, covering her braids, ears and neck and leaving her face neatly framed by a smooth oval. The scarf was secured in place using a couple of maroon pins, newly and brightly bejewelled. Layla loved jewellery-making and she had been undeniably the best bejeweller in her class last year, but that was at her old school. She wondered what the kids she would meet on her first day of Year 8 would think of her work with scarf pins.

Feeling good about the situation, Layla stepped back to suss out her handiwork in the reflection.

Hmm. Not quite!

She scowled. Despite what she thought was foolproof wrapping, a couple of tight black curls had escaped from underneath the scarf, ruining the whole formal-and-neat vibe. Tugging, Layla tried to adjust the hijab, but the silky material slipped back over her braids, exposing her entire hairline. Her afro hair was rarely ever well behaved, and today was no exception.

OMG! HAIR! C'mon! Today is an important day! She mentally scolded the rebellious curls. *Stay put and behave, hey?* Talking to her hair always worked. Layla pulled the scarf forward to cover her hairline again. Patting her head, then brushing her hands down the front of her shirt, Layla smiled inwardly. *You got this!* she told herself, and almost completely believed it.

'Layla! Where are you? We are going to be late!' Baba yelled at her from downstairs. Judging by the clattering, her dad was in the kitchen cleaning up after breakfast. Layla hoped he'd packed something delicious for her lunch. She was going to need all the energy she could get. Today was special because it was the first day of school after the summer break. *Deep breath*, Layla told herself in the voice of an aerobics instructor. *Breathe in and out. In and out. You got this, gurl!* She was nervous because today wasn't just *any* first day of school. It was the first day of her *new school*. And that wasn't the only reason her knees were quivering under her pleated maroon skirt. Layla was starting at a fancy new school on the other side of town, where she didn't know a single soul.

Chapter 2

Layla had loved primary school. At the Islamic School of Brisbane – or ISB for short – everyone knew everyone else. It was family, and Layla had known she belonged. The students were from all over the world: India, Fiji, Nigeria, Pakistan (like her best friend, Dina), Lebanon, Jordan, Algeria, Malaysia and South Africa, just to name a few. So Layla, being from Sudan, was not strange at all. And even better – because most families at the school were recent migrants, their parents became friends and the families hung out together *all the time*. Layla would see Dina at school, again at the grocery store after school and then again at mosque in the evening. Sometimes, to top it all off, they'd visit each other's house at the weekend, their parents talking about politics over a barbeque while the two of them were playing with Dina's pet guinea pigs. Dina would be going back to ISB this year, like almost everyone else in class. Layla was the only one leaving for another school, taking on this challenge all by herself.

See, ISB had been great, but Layla wanted something more. She wanted to be a full-on adventurer, travelling the world, exploring new horizons, bejewelling wherever she went. She might be able to help people too: Layla was a pretty good problem-solver, and loved getting involved in sorting out tricky challenges. Whatever it was, she knew that there was a big, wide world out there that she wanted to discover. She would do anything she could to get herself there.

Being a community school, ISB didn't have a lot of money. Students didn't get the chance to travel, try exotic things and have different adventures, but some kids at other schools did. Layla hadn't known this, living in ignorant bliss, until one fateful afternoon last summer.

It had been a Tuesday like many others, the sky clear and crisp in the hours before sunset. Layla and her younger twin brothers went to the neighbourhood park almost every afternoon to play. They usually started on the court, the loud smack of the rubber basketball ringing out against the concrete. Once the twins got tired of being beaten by their elder sister, they tended to run off on to the swings and Layla would take to the trees. Layla loved climbing. She did it every chance she got and would often disappear up trees whenever the family went out to a park at the weekends. Something about looking up at an enormous eucalyptus or paperbark tree and figuring out the best route to the top gave her a sense of achievement like no other. The closest she got was when she nailed a bejewelling project, but even then . . . Climbing trees was like a *proper* adventure. That Tuesday, Layla had tackled the biggest tree in the park: the avocado tree. It was the neighbourhood's pride and joy, and one of the toughest climbing assignments she'd given herself yet. Its branches sprawled across the sky, thick and heavy with the weight of dark green leaves and fruit just starting to ripen. Up Layla went, puffing and determined, her hands gripping the smooth brown trunk as she ascended.

Straddling one of the thickest branches about halfway up, she stumbled across another person with a climbing habit: Adam. Adam was white, much taller and lankier than her, with chocolate brown hair and dirty fingernails. He wore a baggy black Stussy top, and his Nike shoes were so shiny and new Layla swore she could see her own reflection in the white leather. He didn't seem to mind her tattered Kmart sneakers though.

The two became fast friends that afternoon, a sweet, light-filled friendship that lasted all summer. They would chat and play for hours, legs swinging when they sat on their favourite branch of the avocado tree. As night fell, the orchestral singing of the lorikeets cloaked the tree and their silhouettes in a soft, silky darkness. They yakked about school, music, sports, places they'd been and where they wanted to go.

Layla told Adam about one time when they went back to Sudan and the family home was hit by a sandstorm. 'It's like this huuuuuuge cloud of dustiness just rolls over your house, you know?' she said, her arms flailing as she badly attempted to mimic the billowing sand. 'It gets EVERYWHERE. In your nose, mouth, in the air vents in the car, inside of your wardrobe . . . you end up eating sandy dust with your meals for the next week!'

Adam laughed at the idea of eating sand for breakfast. As a comfortable silence settled upon them, he looked up at the sky. 'Laylz, it's getting late. Race you to the bottom?'

'You know I beat you every time, boy!' Layla retorted, her ratty shoes scrambling across the branch, starting the race before Adam had time to finish his sentence. Layla always won, whether it was up the tree, down the tree, across the road to the shops, or just a sprint round the park.

Adam said that he had never met anyone like Layla before; and it wasn't even because she was Muslim, with a scarf and from the Sahara Desert. No, Layla just had this way of telling stories and seeing the world. She was always asking questions, wondering why. Everything was dramatic through Layla's eyes, and Adam loved it. He inhaled stories about her enormous extended family: her gazillion cousins, eccentric aunties and the hilarious conversations she had with her grandmother on the phone every week, conducted at full volume.

'Why is she always yelling at you down the phone?' Adam asked one day, his curiosity getting the better of him. 'Doesn't she know you can use the volume button?'

Layla chuckled, shaking her head. 'It's either because her hearing is bad, or she thinks she has to yell as we're very far away. Or both.'

Adam became part of the family that summer. He joined Layla and her family for Eid. ('It's kind of like Muslim Christmas,' Layla explained.) He learned to eat *kisra* (a thin savoury pancake used as bread). And he even tagged along to a couple of Ozzie's soccer games with her and Dina. Layla was so happy they seemed to get along.

Phew! Now I don't have to pick a bestie – they both are!

Layla sometimes visited Adam's family as well, but they were very different to the rough and tumble of the Hussein household. Everything was quiet, still and very, very clean. Adam was an only child and both of his parents were busy lawyers, so he spent a lot of time on his own. But his life seemed amazing to Layla. When Adam talked about it, she listened intently, eyes wide, her mind blown. Not only did their family go on holiday to places like the Bahamas, but the school he went to was on another level. Adam told her about camps, sports lessons with high-ropes and trampolining, exciting trips. They even had a whole woodwork workshop where you could build anything you wanted. Layla thought it all sounded soooo cool, especially the part about the workshop.

She imagined going to a school like that would be the perfect way to learn about becoming a real adventurer. She could see so much of Australia and learn about building things she'd only dreamed of. She could do all the stuff she just wouldn't have the opportunity to do at ISB.

Layla thought back to when she had wanted to enter the local go-kart-building competition, but wasn't able to because ISB didn't have the space, equipment or tools for her to build one. To be fair, they only got a basketball court when she was in Year 5, so a workshop was probably asking for a lot.

Layla wished things were different.

She had this deep urge to learn how things worked, spending hours on YouTube watching videos that explained everything from how a toilet flushed to how to drill for oil. She dreamed of making videos just like these – running cool experiments like on *Mythbusters*, or going on voyages to wild places, just as Bear Grylls did. Her home experiments were never as good as the YouTube ones: Layla didn't have much at home to make things with, which was why she often settled for making jewellery out of beads, shells, nuts and anything she could find as a compromise. And even though they weren't award-winning pieces, the process always helped soothe her if she was in a bad mood. After she'd had a fight with Ozzie or the twins, she'd run to the bedroom, scramble for her shoebox full of beads and string, sit on her bed and start threading. Concentrating on one thing that required precision made her feel totally calm and focused. Her breathing would slow down, her mind would stop racing and she could then focus her energy entirely on the now: stringing the next bead. It was the same with some of the other things Layla loved to do: climbing the next branch, placing the next Lego piece. In those moments, nothing else mattered but the task at hand. But there was a limit to what she could make with the tools she had at home – the small screwdriver and *shakoosh* she got for her tenth birthday were not quite enough.

Layla imagined all the types of things she could make at a school like Adam's. She wouldn't have to limit herself to jewellery! She'd always wanted to build a treehouse . . .

'Maybe you could come visit the school sometime,' Adam suggested one afternoon as they swung through the avocado tree, startling the resident lorikeets.

'You reckon?' Layla replied breathlessly as she strained for a branch just out of reach.

'Yeah, I'm sure the teachers wouldn't mind, and I can show you the shelf thing I made last year!'

'Yo, that would be sooo dope. I'll ask my parents for sure!' Grinning, Layla let her mind wander. What would the school look like? What would the workshop *smell* like?

What will people think of me?

The last thought nagged at her momentarily before Layla willed her mind to push the feeling aside. *No time for that kind of thinking.*

Layla bolted home that evening, bursting with energy. Her dark blue mini hijab almost slipped off her head in her excitement.

'ʒ*indi FIKRA!*' she'd announced loudly in Arabic as she'd barrelled through the back door, clutching her headscarf as it slid down her head (again). 'I have an idea!' she'd yelled, and her parents patiently smiled, waiting for Layla to calm down.

'*Barraʒa, barraʒa,*' her mother cooed, soothing her excitable daughter.

Layla threw herself on the stool at the vinyl kitchen bench, as her mother stood in a thin blue *jalabeeya* in front of the sink, peeling potatoes for a stew. The hem of the simple Sudanese dress reached just above the ground and rustled when she moved. Fadia – Mama, as Layla called her – was a tall, dark-skinned Sudanese woman, with strong arms, scarred hands and a gentle face. Her hair, covered in public, was always in two thick braids running along the side of her head, reaching all the way down to her waist. Flecks of grey had started to appear in Fadia's curls, and she had fashioned them into her look, giving her the appearance of a salt-and-pepper warrior queen.

Layla had yet to meet a woman more awesome than her mama (even if she was terrified of her about half the time!). Doctora Fadia was how she was known. Nobody messed with the Doctora.

Baba sat next to Layla at the kitchen bench, chopping tomatoes for the salad. Kareem was shorter than his wife and lighter skinned – his family's tribe was from a different part of Sudan, so whereas Fadia's face was soft curves, Kareem's was all angles: a sharp square jaw, sharp cheekbones, sharp lips. Tight black curls covered his head, dense like sponge, and he wore thick black-framed glasses – glasses that were now sliding down his nose, as they always did when he was cooking. Kareem used his shoulder to push the glasses back up, and then spoke: *'Aha yallah, guuli lehyna. Fikratik shinu?'* He asked Layla to share the idea she was so excited about, the bemused look on his face accompanied by a twitch of his impressive moustache.

Layla explained that Adam said that she could visit his school and check out the workshop. Maybe she could convince the teachers there to let her start making things at their workshop after school? As the words tumbled out of her mouth, she saw her parents look at each other, their glances carrying a meaning unintelligible to Layla. *SIGH.* She knew they were communicating a secret, silent adult understanding she couldn't access, like sending text messages to each other's brain using some adults-only Wi-Fi.

'Well, actually, *habibti*, we have talked to Adam's parents about the different private schools in the city. It turns out that if you work really hard and sit a really difficult exam, you could get a scholarship, which pays for the school fees and would let you *attend* the school itself!' her mother said, eyes dancing. 'Baba and I have been talking about it and agreed that considering another school might be a good idea, if you really want to follow some of these dreams you keep talking about, adventures and whatnot. We know Ozzie decided to stay at ISB, but you don't have to if you don't want to any more.'

'What do you think?' Baba asked, as they both turned to look at her.

Layla stared at her parents, not believing her ears. 'ME? Go to a fancy school?!'

Her parents nodded at her encouragingly.

'OMG. Yes, of course!' Layla jumped off the stool, squealing with delight, before scrambling for her phone to send Adam a message with the news.

As the weeks of summer, autumn then winter went by, Layla studied – harder than she'd ever studied before. In the end, she resorted to the toughest tool in her arsenal: *Shutdown Mode.*

Layla's Shutdown Mode had been famous at ISB – it was how she'd stayed at the top of the class, although Dina often got close. She would be cruising along, laughing and joking with everyone else, and then something would trigger her intense mode and that would be the end of the good times for that week. Or, sometimes, even that whole term.

Layla would become fully focused, going to the library at lunch, rushing to her desk when she got home to continue working on an assignment, not even answering her DMs straight away. Her classmates were quite terrified of Shutdown Mode because it was like Layla turned into a different person. She didn't even smile properly. But in Layla's mind, *You gotta do what you gotta do.* Given this scholarship was so important, Shutdown Mode made the most sense. She had a tough goal: score in the top two per cent of the state. But if she made it, it would be worth it. She would qualify for a fully paid spot at one of the best schools in Queensland.

Dina offered advice and support throughout via a daily stream of motivational pics and gifs to Layla's Tumblr account. It was the only social media Layla allowed herself during SD Mode, and her bestie's love kept her grounded.

Adam was also being supportive but had some bad news. Sadly, if Layla did get into the new school, her new best friend wouldn't be there: his family were moving away at the end of the summer because his mother had got a high-flying job in New York. The thought of Adam's absence made Layla sad, but it wasn't enough to dull her focus and excitement about the adventure ahead. So she ploughed on . . .

I really hope I make this happen! Layla prayed. *Allah, give me strength!* Not a single prayer that year went by without Layla asking God for a little bit of extra support to get through this exam.

The day before the test, Dina dropped a handwritten letter to Layla's house.

If you get this, I will miss you so much at ISB, but I will be so so soooo proud of you. Go show the world what an amazing adventurer you are!

♡ ♡ ♡

With Dina's blessings under her wings, and muttering prayers she'd half made up, Layla strode into that examination room knowing she'd done everything she could to get that scholarship. The rest — well, that was up to Allah.

For weeks, the Hussein family waited with bated breath for the results. The package Layla received was thick and heavy, with her full name embossed on the front in large gold letters: LAYLA KAREEM ABDEL-HAFIZ HUSSEIN.

As she ripped the envelope open, Layla knew that all the hard work had paid off. She had qualified for the scholarship.

OMG YAAAASSSS! THEY AIN'T READY!

Even cooler, the school that she was later accepted to was the best. It was called Mary Maxmillion Grammar School, one of those names that even tasted luxurious when you said it.

Mary Maxmillion Grammar. Layla rolled the syllables around in her mouth as she went to sleep that night, dreaming of the rich, thick, lush grass of the school's front oval. She'd seen the oval in the school's brochure, pictured behind an entrance that was guarded by tall wrought-iron gates that touched the sky.

MMGS was her first step to achieving her dreams of being a *real* adventurer. Climbing the avocado tree was going to be *nothing*!

The new school uniform included a cream straw hat, which was giving Layla grief. She tried to squeeze the un-hijab-friendly piece on top of her headscarf, but it looked ridiculous. She giggled self-consciously. Oh yeah, that was the other thing. Layla was going to be the first person *ever* to wear a headscarf at MMGS. The only one! WILD!

She had found that out during the acceptance meeting before school started. MMGS had asked Layla and her parents to come to the school, so one balmy evening the family walked in to find a roomful of men in suits sitting round a huge dark mahogany table. The boardroom was intimidating, with large paintings of important-looking old white guys all over the walls. The Hussein family dutifully took their seats, and the man at the head of the table did most of the talking. He had a very powerful-sounding title, 'Chair of the Board', and proceeded to inform

Layla in a booming voice that she would be getting a scholarship and *would* be allowed to wear the hijab, even though he personally wasn't a supporter of this policy.

Layla rolled her eyes, wondering why he had to make such a big deal about it. Her headscarf even matched the school colours perfectly!

'This is *not* a Muslim school, this is an Australian school. You should follow the way *we* do things,' Mr Cox had announced in a deep, sonorous voice.

A softer voice interrupted, gently challenging the Chair. 'As principal, I have the last say on admissions and given your excellent results, we have awarded you a full scholarship, and so you and your family are very welcome at this school.' Layla turned to look at the principal – a small, balding man – regarding her kindly.

'Tyrone Savage is my name. Hopefully not my game though,' he said, a smile playing across his lips. 'Welcome again, to our wonderful education facility. Any questions?'

After the formalities of the meeting, Layla was cornered by Mr Cox. She was in the middle of wrapping up a biscuit in a napkin and stuffing it in her pocket for later when he walked up to her.

'Congratulations on being allowed into this school,' he said, his moustache bristling. He leaned in, menacingly. 'Remember to behave, because we can cancel your scholarship at any time.' He faced away from Layla but whispered into her ear. 'You're a *brave* young girl, to do what you're doing. Not everyone at MMGS is as excited as Mr Savage to have you around.' Mr Cox straightened his jacket before walking away.

Layla didn't know whether to laugh with excitement or cry in fear. Was that a warning? A threat? What was she supposed to do? She couldn't really tell. She didn't feel like telling anyone about it just yet though. She was sure she'd be able to figure it out.

Well, at least everyone will know me!

Anyway, what was she doing to be brave? Was it really brave to be herself? You'd think that'd be the easiest thing to be.

Chapter 3

'LAYLA!' Baba bellowed again from downstairs. She heard the car engine start. 'I'm going to leave without you!'

Oh no! Layla threw the straw hat on the bed. It wasn't going to fit on her headscarf, and who wears hats anyway? She grabbed her backpack, stumbled clumsily over her skirt as she ran down the stairs and into the kitchen to get her lunchbox, then she bolted into the garage just as her dad was pulling out, almost tripping over the shoes in front of the door. 'Waaaaiiiittttt!'

Ozzie was sitting in the front seat, laughing as she opened the back door of the car and clambered in. 'We were gonna leave you!' he sang with glee.

OMG! Ozzie was so annoying. He was in Year 11, but Layla swore he acted like a two-year-old most of the time. Her eldest brother looked most like Baba – lean body, light brown skin, spongy black hair, strong jawline – but he was going to be much taller. He was already as tall as their dad. The height came from their mother's genes, as Fadia often reminded them.

Layla shot her older brother a dirty look then slammed the door of the white Camry, hard. Ozzie jumped, and she chuckled. *Serves him right!* Her younger brothers, though, were not so pleased. Sami and Yousif were being crushed by her backpack and were squealing with annoyance.

'Layla, you're squishing me!' Sami groaned.

The bag was heavy with her new textbooks, so he was not totally out of line. The twins looked like stretched toddlers – gangly limbs, huge dark brown eyes and the signature Hussein curls that Fadia kept trimmed short.

'*Ya-nhar-abyad*,' Layla muttered under her breath – using a curse word that only grandmothers used – then shifted the bag to her lap. Comfortable, she turned to the window, feeling the air on her face and through her headscarf as the Hussein crew backed out of the garage and sped off.

Layla was the last one in the car, after Ozzie and the twins had been dropped off at ISB in the next suburb. This new school was half an hour away, out of the suburbs and set among the hills and high-rises of the inner city. Baba pulled over at the gate and parked in the crowded bay area out the front of the school.

Ya-nhar-aswad! she whispered, using another curse word reserved for grandmothers. She liked using curse words that were a little unusual – it felt like her own secret language.

The place was really out of control! It was dark when they'd last visited, so Layla hadn't really seen the school in its full glory. In the sunlight though . . . *whoa*.

The buildings behind the tall gate were like something out of a Harry Potter movie. Sandstone with huge glass windows; the front entry looked like the *actual* stairway to heaven. Layla could see the large green oval in the distance. ISB, with its temporary-feeling shipping-container rooms and nothing over one storey tall, looked like a children's playground compared to this place.

'Good luck today, Layla,' Baba called from the driver's seat. 'Do your best. Show them how smart the Hussein family is! Try not to get into trouble.'

Layla chuckled as she waved at the car, then she turned to the front gate and took a huge, deep breath. *You got this*, Layla told herself, as she adjusted her backpack and walked through the gates.

Kids milled around her, chatting excitedly about their holidays. 'Oooooooohhhhhh!' she heard one girl screech to another. 'Look at your hair!'

'Oh, man, you look like you've been working out,' a deeper voice behind her said, in what Layla assumed was a conversation between two rugby players.

'OMG, Sarah totally hooked up with that boy from the party. He's sooo fine!'

Layla had no idea what everyone was talking about, but she knew she'd figure it out. That's what made adventures fun!

Walking through the throngs of students, she felt a hush falling around her as she passed groups of people.

Layla's eyes darted from side to side, not wanting to draw any extra attention to herself, but it was too late. The eyes of hundreds of curious, hostile and confused kids – and some parents and teachers – followed her down the path as she walked towards the largest structure she could see. She approached what appeared to be the main reception building to ask for directions. Walking up the path, she clocked three girls standing in front of the glass doors and gulped. *Please don't notice me*, she prayed, eyes shut tight for a short moment. *Allah, help a sister out!*

The girls were skinny and pretty and, gosh, did they know it – their shiny blonde hair gleamed and their school skirts that looked way too short to be regulation. Wow, those legs! How were they so smooth? And shiny? Layla was glad her brown hairy legs were covered by the skirt. Even looking at the girls made Layla feel uncool. She glanced down as she walked past the group and towards the door. Layla concentrated on her shoes, one step in front of the other. *SLAM!* A loud bang interrupted her. *Ohhhhhhhhhh . . .*

Looking down meant Layla hadn't quite seen the door. She had walked right into the glass pane! Her head throbbed as the entire door shook, and the three girls nearby whipped round to stare at Layla, their perfect noses delicately scrunched in mocking laughter. Layla shook her head and stared straight ahead, desperately trying to pretend that nothing had happened.

The beautiful girls weren't going to let her get off that easily, though.

'Hahaha! Watch where you're going, you freak! Who are you, anyway?' the tallest girl spat out, her words hitting Layla like shards.

One of the other girls good-naturedly pushed her friend on the shoulder. 'Don't be so mean, Veronica! Leave the poor refugee girl alone, she looks terrified!'

They all laughed and turned away, forgetting the new student almost instantly.

Layla shook her head, looked at the sky and muttered to her God. *Allah! Where were you?! Rah*, MMGS was going to be some hard work.

★

It took Layla *forever* to find her classroom. She was in 8A.

A for Awesome, she had said to herself when she found out, chuckling a little, the door incident forgotten. She had sung a little hype-up tune to make herself feel better, and her jokes did the same, working their magic on her mood. She could make herself laugh for ages with her lame jokes, which had earned her the nickname Broken Record at her old school. Layla wondered if her classmates here would think she was funny.

Humming, Layla threw her schoolbag on the rack outside her classroom. The bulging maroon backpack lay precariously on top of the untidy pile of identical bags. She then pushed the door and walked into the classroom.

The room fell silent, and everyone turned to look at her. The humming caught in her throat, and she paused just inside the doorway, wondering if she'd done something wrong, again. Was it because she'd forgotten the hat? Dammit! Or had class already started? The clock on the wall said 8.40 a.m.! *Rah*, how long had she been lost for?

'Ah, come on in. You must be Layla. Now that everyone is here, we can finally get started. Layla, would you like to take a seat?' The thin voice came from the front of the room.

Everyone turned to look at the teacher. At first Layla couldn't tell if the teacher was friendly or annoyed, though her narrowing eyes gave her away. A moment later, everyone turned back to Layla. It was almost like a tennis match. The woman standing at the front of the classroom had a scarily wrinkled face, a little like a prune. Her eyes were beady, framed by trendy cat-eye glasses. Her lips were painted a shockingly bright pink, which popped against her pale skin. She had broad shoulders and very thin legs, with straight white hair that was pulled up in a tight, tight bun. Layla wondered if the hairstyle gave her headaches. Sometimes when she tied her headscarf too tight it gave her these wicked migraines . . .

'Ahem.' The teacher made another noise, startling Layla out of her thoughts.

'Oh . . . y-y-yup,' Layla croaked. She cleared her throat. She could do better than this. 'YUP! I'M

LAYLA!' she yelled. Uh-oh. Too loud. Why weren't her vocal cords cooperating today? A couple of people snickered. 'Sorry for yelling, Miss,' she said. 'I just wanted to make sure you could hear me. I've had a weird morning, you know? I ran into a door . . . anyway.' Layla took in a deep breath. When she was flustered, she could ramble. What was she even saying? Oh yes. She should apologize for yelling. 'Well, you see, sorry for yelling, because, like, well –' *Think of an excuse, quick!* – 'I have to yell at my grandma when I'm on the phone with her because she's a bit deaf and you kind of remind me of my grandma so I thought I should yell. Just in case. I was just being polite, you know.'

The class erupted with laughter.

Oh no.

'I mean – I don't mean you're old, Miss, I meant to say, like, my grandma's really wise and kind, you know . . .'

The teacher's face was darkening with anger, and Layla slowly spluttered to a stop. As the class continued to roar, Layla grimaced. She'd really put her foot in it, making fun of the teacher straight away. What had got into her? She was usually pretty good at talking to adults, even if they didn't like her, but maybe it was the nerves? Like, she knew that sometimes her hijab made old people act weird around her – Mr Cox was one example – even people on the street stared at her a bit, but she usually knew how to handle it. Maybe she really had hit her head hard on that door.

'Janey Mack!' Layla muttered an old Irish saying under her breath, one she'd learned to use instead of swearing. Why did she let her mouth run off like that? This was such a disaster.

But maybe she could fix it!

'Oh, Miss, I'm so sorry. I meant no disrespect – you're really beautiful for an elderly woman.'

Elderly woman? JANEY MACK, Layla, what has gotten into you?! Layla couldn't believe the words coming out of her own mouth.

The teacher's brown beady eyes had narrowed again, and her pink lips had been pressing tighter and tighter together – you could barely see them any more, they were just two pink lines underneath a flat

33

nose. With this final sentence from Layla, the teacher snapped.

'Layla! This is *completely* unacceptable! I beg your pardon! We will not have any of that disrespectful attitude in this school, thank you very much! I don't care where you've come from, but rest assured behaviour like that won't be acceptable here.'

'Where I've come from?' Layla paused. What did she mean? 'You mean, like, from my mother?'

The class laughed louder, and Layla smiled uncertainly. She didn't even think that was a very good joke, really. Ah well, she might have got off on the wrong foot with the teacher, but at least her classmates knew she was funny. Hehe.

'OK, OK, I'm just going to . . .' Deciding to move out of the line of fire, Layla scrambled to find a spare seat, glancing around the class, trying to make eye contact with someone, anyone, for permission. A girl with blonde frizzy hair smiled at Layla cautiously, but there were no spare seats round her. Layla finally spotted one right at the back of the class and made her way to the last available seat in 8A, squeezing into a plastic chair in the corner. There were two boys on either side of her.

'I'm Ethan,' said one, his greeny-hazel eyes piercing Layla's soul. Layla felt her heart skip a beat, maybe two, and her breath caught in her throat. *Who is this guy?*

'And I'm Seb,' said the other before she could respond. Seb looked Latino, with overgrown dark wavy hair that covered his eyes.

Layla nodded at them both, and she settled into her seat and pulled out her laptop.

'That was pretty funny, the way you shut Ms Taylor down,' Ethan said, after a few moments of silence, and Seb nodded. 'Nice one, hey.'

Both boys put their hands up for a high five and Layla hit both of them at the same time before winking. She thought that Ethan was kind of cute – red hair, crooked teeth and freckles. School might be all right after all . . .

'Layla!' the teacher yelled from the front of the class. 'Eyes to the front! If I get any more rude behaviour from you, I *will* be contacting your parents!'

Layla was startled by the threat. Maybe she could get away with one more joke. This one always went down so well at ISB . . .

'Miss, is it because I'm black?'

Ms Taylor's face looked like she was going to explode.

'OUT! GET . . . OUT . . . NOW!'

Chapter 4

Layla collapsed on to the wooden bench outside the classroom door and stared out at the brick courtyard, stunned. She couldn't believe she'd been kicked out of her first class on her first day of school. *Rah*. She liked being cheeky, but it didn't usually get her into *that* much trouble. MMGS was next level. She was supposed to come in, make some friends and have some adventures — not get kicked out of class. She shook her head vigorously, trying to clear her thoughts and wondering where it had all gone wrong.

Maybe I just got too excited, or nervous?

Layla knew that sometimes her mouth operated before her brain had processed everything, and the results weren't always great. Like, well, right now. As the reality of what had just happened sank in, she started to feel sick to her stomach, gritting her teeth tightly and squeezing her eyes closed until her eyelids flipped inside out.

Ya Allah! *What about the scholarship?! Is this going to mess things up?* Ya-nhar-abyad, *why does my mouth get me into so much trouble?*

Layla thought of all the disagreements at the dinner table at home, or that time a lady called the police at the bus stop when Layla told her to stop staring at her hijab. *I still think that was funny.* Layla smiled to herself, momentarily losing herself in the memory.

Maybe, maybe if she held her breath for ten seconds with her eyes closed, she would wake up from this crazy dream. Layla started counting down. *Ten Mississippi, nine Mississippi, eight Mississippi . . .*

Layla opened her eyes. *Still here.* The wooden bench felt hard underneath her body, offering no comfort, and the humid summer air pressed against her skin. Layla wasn't the type to worry much, but as she thought about what might happen, a strange feeling crept over her body. She gritted her teeth — *no, no, no* — but it was too late. Her stomach began to churn and Layla convulsed, a violent sensation shooting up her oesophagus. She clenched her jaw to try to stop the inevitable. Her chest started heaving.

Janey Mack, I need to get out of here before I spew everywhere!

A few minutes later Layla returned to the bench sheepishly, having vomited her breakfast in a bush. She wiped her mouth with the inside of her sleeve and grimaced. She wondered if she now smelled of sick. *Probably.* She was pretty sure smelling of spew would ruin all the street cred she'd gained by this point. Layla slumped lower on the bench, her mind a noisy jumble. Her long maroon skirt billowed around her, showing off her ankles. *And my legs aren't even properly moisturized!* Her skin was ashy, dry from the lack of any cream or Vaseline, which Sudanese women use daily to keep their skin supple. Mama was always banging on about moisturizing, but it just made Layla feel sticky.

Even the softest skin wasn't going to be enough to save her halal bacon now. Ignoring the fact that she'd just been sick from the tension, what would Mama and Baba do when they heard about this? Would this mean she would lose her scholarship? Baba had always said her 'long tongue' would get her into trouble. She needed to find a way to fix this. Closing her eyes, Layla took slow, careful breaths. '*Bismillah, Alhamdulillah, Allah-hu-Akbar*.' Layla repeated a *dua* that helped her calm down, and then turned her mind to What She Needed To Do To Fix This (thinking in capital letters helps).

OK. Firstly, Ms Taylor's good books. She had to prove herself! She didn't want people to think she was a mean person, that was definitely pretty un-Islamic. Plus, she needed to behave otherwise they'd take the scholarship from her, like Mr Cox had threatened!

Maybe she could bake a cake. LOL, nah, she always made a mess cooking anything, and her mum would smack her bottom with the *mufrak* – a wooden Sudanese cooking implement used for making the traditional dish *mulaa7*. *What else?* Layla thought while she stroked her imaginary beard, pretending she was a famous old man philosopher like Aristotle or Ibn Batuta. Maybe she could give Ms Taylor one of those cool glass-bead necklaces she had learned to make over the summer. Or maybe offer to bejewel her phone?

Then Layla remembered the feeling of having everyone in the class laugh at her jokes. Man, being funny felt *good*. A smile crept on to her face at the memory. Maybe she could try again to make Ms Taylor laugh. *Hehe*. Layla imagined Ms Taylor's wrinkly face laughing at one of her jokes. What a sight that would be! Sighing, Layla shifted her weight, trying to avoid touching the traces of vomit on her sleeve.

BRIIIIINGGGGGG! The bell's piercing note rang across the courtyard, and Layla's eyes snapped open. Janey Mack! She had fallen asleep! Layla quickly wiped up a bit of drool that had seeped out of her mouth. *I hope no one saw me!* Layla looked around furtively, but there was no one in sight, only the rustle of the breeze through the eucalyptus trees. Layla straightened up on the bench, rearranged the skirt to cover her ashy ankles and waited. Almost immediately, the class doors opened. Ethan and Seb were the first two out, bolting from the air-conditioned room like they were being chased by a rhino. Ethan was the first to spot her on the bench and skipped excitedly over, plopping himself next to the still-sleepy Layla. Seb followed, sitting on her other side. Ms Taylor walked out behind them, surrounded by a sea of Layla's new classmates. The homeroom teacher made her way over and stood in front of the bench, her broad-shouldered silhouette looming large in front of Layla. 'I won't be taking any more action on this incident today, young lady,' she said, her voice tight. 'However, consider this a warning. I suggest you reflect on your behaviour, and the kind of reputation you'd like at this school. Now.' The older woman took her hands off her hips and gestured out. 'Go on and enjoy your recess.'

The boys on either side of Layla, silent during the confrontation, both turned to her as soon as Ms Taylor had walked away. 'C'mon, Layla, come on, come hang with us today!' Ethan grinned at her, bubbling excitedly. 'You gotta meet the rest of the crew!'

'Yeh, you're pretty cool for a girl!' said Seb. 'So, you can come hang with us!'

'Cool. I'll get my food out of my bag, and let's go!' she said.

Layla was pleased. She wasn't expecting to find friends so quickly, and these boys were so different to her friends back at primary school, but that could be fun, right? They smelled of adventure, and Layla liked adventure. They also smelled of trouble (and, maybe, weird stinky body odour? Or was that deodorant? Lynx?) but Layla wasn't bothered.

I can handle myself. Layla was sure that wasn't a lie. Well, pretty sure. She felt a creeping sliver of doubt but pushed it right back down.

The blonde girl from class had also walked out and was rummaging in her bag while Layla looked for her bag. When the girl turned round, packet of chips in hand, she introduced herself.

'Nice hijab,' she said, her voice low and sweet. She pronounced the 'h' in a way that showed she clearly spoke Arabic. 'My mum's Muslim, so she wears one just like it.' The girl gently offered Layla a smile before looking back down at the ground.

Receiving the smile with grace, Layla responded in kind, with a toothy grin. 'Oh, that's awesome!' she said, secretly relieved that she hadn't frightened everyone in the class away. 'What's your name? Do you want to come hang out with me and the boys?'

The girl's head jerked backwards, as she shook her head vehemently, her blonde curls bouncing in her ponytail. 'Oh no, no, no, that's cool. I'm cool just chilling here. Thanks, though. Oh, and my name's Leesa by the way.' The girl fiddled with the bag of chips in her hands nervously. 'Nice to meet you. Bye, *salams*! Oh – and watch out, I think someone vomited in a bush or something, there's a weird smell over there.'

Layla watched Leesa walk away, wondering how different things would be if she'd ended up sitting next to her in class.

Thank God she doesn't think I was the one who vomited . . . phew!

'C'mon, Laylz, let's go!' the boys called.

The three took off running, Seb's dark brown hair flopping as they trotted round the back of the building towards the grassy hill behind the classroom. A group of Year 8 lads were lounging on the grass at the top of the hill, a collection of grey shorts, sagging socks and untucked blue shirts. Half the boys had already loosened their ties, and a few even had their shirts unbuttoned! *Cheeky!*

Layla took in the sight before her. She'd thought MMGS was going to be super white. The group they were walking towards wasn't quite what she'd expected: they were almost as mixed-looking as the kids from ISB! That was kinda cool. Maybe she wouldn't feel so out of place here after all.

As they started up the hill, the three slowed to a walk. Seb turned to Layla. 'What are you eating today?' he asked.

'Oh – um – I – um – I didn't bring any food for morning tea today . . .' Layla stuttered, momentarily caught off guard. The lies tumbled out of her mouth awkwardly. She felt comfortable with these boys, but she knew they weren't ready for Baba's weird Sudanese experiments that he considered 'food' just yet. She really wanted to impress them, so hadn't even bothered to collect any food from her bag, not after she'd seen Leesa with those fancy organic chips. Baba had made one of his infamous honey-and-Nutella sandwiches. They were maybe the most acceptable of Baba's experiments, but Layla *hated* them. They got soggy in the cling film, seeped out dark sticky goo and made the bread resemble something a dog had vomited up. He'd also packed one of those homemade yoghurt tubs, which used to stink up the entire ISB playground back in primary school. The Greek yoghurt her father preferred tasted and smelled like half a kilo of old feta cheese mixed with yellow bird doo-doo. *Sigh*. She'd have to have a conversation with Baba when she got home . . . *Oh, wait. I just got kicked out of class.* Maybe she wouldn't mention his food *just* yet.

'What about you guys?' she asked, trying to forget about the trouble she'd be in tonight.

'Ethan gets a feed from the tuckshop every day,' Seb said. 'He's pretty lucky!'

Ethan's head was down, and he mumbled a response. 'Ya, well, ya know, Mum and Dad are busy and don't have time to make me stuff. It's, like, whatever.' He fiddled with a cling-film-wrapped chocolate muffin in his hands, the price tag still visible.

'Nah, it's cool, you know I got ya, bro.' Seb laughed. 'And you know you can always come to mine. Mum *loves* feeding ya!' Seb shoved Ethan in his back good-naturedly, making him chuckle.

Seb turned to Layla. 'My ma is Colombian, and she loves feeding all my mates. She gives me the tastiest food for lunch, and if I don't eat it, I'll get whooped! But it's a win for me, cos it's suuuuuper tasty!' Seb chuckled.

By this point, they had reached the top of the hill. Layla tried to hide her panting. All this exercise, and in this loooong skirt! Gosh, the hill hadn't looked this steep when they were at the bottom. From this vantage point though, they could see over almost the entire school. Layla looked around her, taking it all in and gasping in awe. There was so much green, more shades than she knew names for. The sun glinted off the glass and steel of the school buildings couched in among the trees, and, in the distance, you could see the high-rises of the city centre. The school brochures didn't do this place justice.

'It's all right, hey?' Ethan asked Layla quietly as they stood next to each other, surveying the landscape. Layla nodded, staring at her classmate out of the corner of her eye. Ethan's auburn hair was slicked back, and his freckles popped against his pale white skin, a fiery constellation on high cheekbones. A single red curl fell out of the neatly combed arrangement on Ethan's head, obscuring his eye. He brushed it aside gently and smiled at Layla self-consciously.

Layla blushed and looked away. *Did we just have a moment?!* She'd read about instances like these in magazines, but this was the first time she'd actually *felt* one. *My whole stomach just flipped!*

Fortunately, no one was paying the pair any attention. Seb was busy throwing himself on the ground, opening his A4-sized blue lunchbox and breathing in the funkalicious smell that drifted across the grassy hill. The stench was so thick that Layla turned round and swore she could almost see the bits of garlic wafting up from the Tupperware container. At the smell, the boys groaned in unison.

'You love it!' Seb boasted to the group, smiling.

The moans only grew louder, and Layla smiled too. They were kinda like her family, teasing each other all the time! She got it.

Taking a spoonful of the rice and meat concoction into his mouth, Seb waved his free hand, introducing Layla. He spat out bits of food as he talked. 'All right, boys, meet Layla! She *totally* shut Ms Taylor down in class – she was all like "Is it cos I'm black?" and Ms T went WILD and threw her out!'

'*Ohhhhhhh!*' The motley crew laughed and jeered in response to the story.

Standing at the edge of the group, Layla had been nervous, her mouth as dry as the Sahara Desert she was born in. With Seb's hyping, though, and the reaction from the boys, Layla beamed with joy, basking in their admiration. *They might actually like me!*

'Oh, you know, it was nothing.' She looked down at the ground with fake humility, smiling to herself.

Seb continued. 'Right then, Layla, this is Baz – short for Barak, the original Obama; Scotty; Gordon and Tony – full name Antonio, like in the Mafia, but we all call him Tony.'

Layla knew that this was a big moment: her first introduction to the posse.

OK, OK. I got this. I just need to make them laugh or something, right?

Layla steeled herself, her heart beating so loudly that she was surprised no one had made a joke about the marching band practising round the corner. Pulling her hands out of her pockets and placing them on her hips, she struck a pose and tried to channel her inner Cardi B.

'Right, anyway. I heard you were the cool kids in town, but I guess that was wrong, ay?'

The boys all looked up at her, staring. There was a moment of silence.

OMG. IT DIDN'T WORK. I AM ACTUALLY GOING TO DIE!

Then, the tension snapped, and the boys' faces split into smiles and they laughed. 'Oh yeh, funny one, Laylz!' someone yelled above the din.

Layla had to stop herself falling over with relief. She'd guessed it was just like with Ozzie and you just had to tease them to make them laugh. *Alhamdulillah*, her guess had worked out! This was definitely a new experience: she had never really been friends with the boys back at her old school. The only boy she'd ever been friends with was Adam. At primary school, all her friends were girls, including her bestie, Dina. It wasn't that she didn't like the boys, but the ones at ISB were all a bit gross, and she'd known them for, like, her *whole life*. She'd seen them pick their noses and wet their shorts. They were like brothers. But these boys seemed more interesting, and Layla had always been curious to know what it would be like to hang out with the cool kids.

The conversation continued around her, and Layla almost felt like she was in a documentary that followed different creatures in their natural habitats! *I'll pretend I'm that Daniel Attenborough guy – or is it David Attenborough?*

The bell rang for class, jarring Layla out of her daydream. Off they trudged back to 8A.

'Oi, wait. So why do you look like you're a nun, by the way?' Tony jokingly asked Layla, his grin reflecting his light tone. 'Or one of those blackies that hang out near that funny-looking building in Holland Park?'

Layla laughed, but carefully, slightly nervous again. She'd known this was coming. 'Mate, nobody says "blackie". Dude, is this 1950? I'm a Muzzo! Muslim, actually. Ya know?' she replied, her voice teasing but pointed, sharpened by hurt. Layla raised her eyebrows and Tony looked slightly ashamed.

'Oh, sorry, I didn't mean it in any bad way or anything . . .' As his voice trailed off, Layla smiled cautiously and started to twirl, letting her skirt fly up like an umbrella. She had been slightly worried about what people would say about her wearing the hijab at her new school, and she'd considered starting at MMGS without it. But after talking it through with her mother, she'd realized that wasn't a good enough reason, really.

'Just remember why you decided to start wearing it,' Layla's mum had said to her. 'If you really want to take it off, that's up to you. But remember, if you're wearing it for the sake of Allah, he always has your back.'

Layla had nodded, still nervous, but determined to push through.

And now, look! I'm twirling! It's not so bad after all!

'And because I get to do cool things like thi–' As she danced in front of Tony, Layla was cut off by a hard-edged voice.

'You're like one of those terrorists that are always yelling "durka durka" on the news, aren't you?'

The question rang through the air, the accusation cracking like a whip. Silence fell upon the group. Layla turned to find the owner of the voice. Her gaze settled on the boy and their eyes locked – hers dark brown and steady, his piercing turquoise and sharp. Layla knew this boy was trouble. He had been sitting near them on the hill. Tall, with brooding eyes and a platinum-white mop of hair, the guy had a weird vibe about him.

'Peter Cox,' Ethan whispered, under his breath.

Layla shook her head, shaking off the chill she felt, then forced a laugh.

'Ha-ha! Yup, that's me,' Layla smiled toothlessly at the boy, trying to lighten things up, but his face didn't change.

Hmm, he thinks he's so hard. All right then! Layla smirked, but her face darkened and became intensely serious. She used one of the tricks she'd seen her older brother muster when he was hassled by people in the park while playing basketball.

'You better be careful not to make me angry, Peter. Otherwise . . .' Layla took a step towards the boy. She felt a strange sense of satisfaction as she saw his face betray a slight trace of fear.

'Otherwise . . .' Her voice softened as she repeated the word.

'I'm going to blow . . .' Another step.

'You . . .' The words came out of her mouth slowly.

'Up.'

She took a final step towards Peter, their faces almost touching. She could feel his breath on her face, hot and fast. His pupils were huge, the blues of his irises almost invisible.

'BOOM!' she then thundered, powerfully and loud.

Peter jumped almost a foot in the air, making a noise like a strangled cat.

'Gotcha!' Layla sneered, as the rest of the boys around her began to cackle.

Layla breathed a sigh of relief. She didn't like picking fights with people – that was always too much drama, and she'd usually moved on by the time things got to the fight stage – but she knew that if she showed a bully that she wasn't scared, they would usually leave her alone.

And it doesn't hurt that it made the other boys laugh!

Layla twirled away from Peter with a flourish, poking her tongue out and winking at him cheekily. '*Yallah*. Let's go, boys!' she yelled at her newfound clique before skipping away from the stunned bully.

'What class do we have now?' Layla turned to Ethan and Seb as the group began dispersing to their various classes, Peter still standing by himself on the hill.

'Oh, hmm. I think we have design and tech! Yaass!' Seb replied. 'Oh, and don't worry about him –' Seb pointed back over his shoulder to Peter – 'he's in a different class. He's a bit of a loner. Nobody really talks to him or pays him much attention anyway.'

Layla nodded (*Alhamdulillah!*), then turned to Ethan. 'Is tech like woodwork class?' She hoped it was. Layla could barely contain her excitement.

'It's, like, building things. It's super fun, we just get to muck around with tools all class and make really cool stuff.'

'Yeh, and we can play whatever music we want too! It's so good!'

'AND Mr Gilvarry lets us get away with heeeaaps.' Ethan smiled at Layla, who could barely contain her glee.

YAAAAS! FINALLY! This is my time to shine.

Tech class, as they called it, was in a building on the outskirts of the school, across the oval. They trudged across the field, passing bad jokes and banter back and forth around the group like a football. Eventually, they reached the building.

'C'mon, it's on the top floor!'

The group climbed the stairs. Layla trailed her hand along the wall, feeling the cool concrete against her fingertips. At the top there was a long hall, and at the far end stood Mr Gilvarry, leaning in the tech-room doorway.

'Welcome!' Mr Gilvarry had a huge belly and an even larger moustache. His red beard was full and bushy and looked like it had never, *ever* seen a comb. He reminded Layla of a jolly bus driver.

As the students milled about the room, Layla slowed to a walk and took in the scene in front of her. The workshop smelled like an industrious combination of pine, wood shavings and varnish. The room was filled with rows of wooden workbenches with dark yellow clamps on each edge. The back wall was covered in hand tools of every shape and size: hammers, screwdrivers, chisels, saws, planes . . . and a whole bunch of things she had never seen before. On the right-hand side of the room stood a large bench saw, bandsaw and router, and on the other side stood a number of wooden sculptures that looked like they were previous students' works. It was magical. The roof was made from glass, so the sun shone in brightly, lighting the workshop like a showroom. OMG – there were even a couple of digital 3D printers in the corner!

Layla couldn't stop herself from squealing. *Are we going to be allowed to use all these machines to make things?*

She could print off cool-shaped beads and jewellery with that printer for a start, and maybe even make some nice wooden jewellery boxes. Gosh, she definitely could have made a go-kart for that competition if she had been allowed to use all this stuff. And, mate, there were enough tools in here that she might even be able to build that treehouse! So many possibilities!

Mr Gilvarry leaned on a workbench, smiling at the excitement Layla wore on her face. 'Young lady, welcome to your new home. You're going to build four things this year, one new project every term. You can also come in and use any of the equipment during lunchtimes, and even after school, if you let me know in advance. The workshop is yours – make the most of it!'

This. Is. The. BESTTTT!

Walking to the front gate of the school that afternoon, Layla breathed a sigh of relief. This wasn't so bad. What had she been so worried about this morning? She could fit in to this place, even if she looked a bit different. Actually, she couldn't wait for the year ahead. Hanging out with cool boys, building things, making people laugh, and maybe being able to eat her smelly food in front of everyone else without being embarrassed; this was it. MMGS had been a great idea. She just had one or two problems to sort out first . . . Layla pushed the thought of getting kicked out of class into a little box in her brain, alongside Peter, then slammed it shut.

Focus on this goodness right now, she told herself.

The crowd around her thickened as people started jostling and running towards the bus that had just pulled up. Layla's foot caught on an uneven slab of concrete, and she felt herself flying forward unexpectedly, her face slapping the ground.

Ohhhhh, Janey Mack!

Layla felt her face burn red with embarrassment. She hoped nobody had noticed, but she could feel the eyes of everyone around her. As she pushed herself up into a sitting position, people got out of the way, but nobody really offered to help. *Pretend nothing happened*, Layla told herself, and smiled at the few people who had stopped and were looking at her with sympathetic eyes.

'It's all right. I'm all good! I was just surveying the footpath and needed to get a closer look!' Layla tried a lame joke, forcing herself to sound cheerful even though her hands stung.

Glancing down, Layla located the source of the pain. Her palms were shredded. She shook her hands in front of her, searching for somewhere she could run cool water over her wounds.

As Layla looked around, someone came up behind her, blocking the sunlight. The menacing presence seemed to lean down, then Layla heard a whisper in her ear.

'Get your towelhead face out of our school. In fact, get out of our COUNTRY. You're not welcome here,' the voice uttered, dripping with venom.

Layla whipped round to face her accuser. A boy loomed above her, towering and brooding. His eyebrows were dark and his face was twisted and mean, but the sun was behind him, so Layla couldn't see his features properly.

'You better watch yourself, dirty Ay-raaaab,' he spat, his voice still low to avoid attracting attention from the passers-by.

Behind him stood Peter, and Layla realized why the boy who attacked her seemed familiar. He must be Peter's older brother. Layla's mind raced. *OK, somehow I'm gonna need to really show them that they don't scare me. It's now or never.* Layla braced herself for the uncomfortable moment ahead and stood up. *Just act like you don't even care . . .*

'Hahahahaha!' She forced a laugh out, loud enough for everyone to hear. 'You're calling me a dirty Arab? You can't even say the word right . . . I'm not even really Arab! I'm from Sudan, so I'm African, and I speak Arabic. You can't even insult me right!' Turning her attention away from the older boy, she addressed Peter. 'And you needed your big brother to help you out, Peter? Couldn't even handle me yourself?!' Layla watched Peter's face darken with each word she uttered.

Every dope queen needs an archenemy.

A crowd had gathered round the three students at Layla's loud announcement, the bus schedule all but forgotten. In an effort to keep her quiet, the older boy stepped forward and growled at Layla again. 'SHUT UP!' he warned, eyes wide and darting left to right furtively.

Layla wasn't gonna be silenced. Her parents had taught her to yell in the face of injustice.

'YOU WANT ME TO BE QUIET?' she yelled, throwing her hands up. 'You're the one being mean to me!'

The two boys stood in front of her and Layla's eyes met Peter's. He stepped forward aggressively. *Is he going to touch me?* Layla wondered, the first tendrils of fear creeping into her. *Yo, he looks like he actually wants to hurt me.*

'Your type doesn't belong here!' Peter spat the words out, inches from her face. Then his palms came up and he pushed Layla backwards.

Layla stumbled.

'Why.' *Push.* 'Don't.' *Push.* 'You.' *Push.* 'Just.' *Push.* '*LEAVE!*'

On saying the last word, Peter pushed Layla so hard that she fell off the kerb and right on to her bottom.

There was an eerie silence as Layla looked around. Lots of people were recording the whole thing on their phones. Layla's mind went blank as she sat on the ground, frozen. What on earth was happening? She unthinkingly began to straighten her headscarf, pulling one side down so it was even again. If someone was going to put this on Snapchat – which she knew they would – at least her headscarf should look neat!

'You're not even Australian. Why don't you go back to where you came from?'

With that, Layla snapped. Like hell this kid was going to tell her that she wasn't Australian.

'Oi! I am Australian, you fool! Why don't you go back to where YOU came from, you convict! Why don't you go back to England? Oh yeah, they sent you away – they wouldn't want you back anyway!' For the second time that afternoon, Layla scrambled to her feet. This time, however, she walked right up to Peter and, without thinking, closed her eyes, then jerked her head forward and *headbutted him*.

Peter dropped like a sack of potatoes, and the crowd broke out into chaotic jeers and screams.

Layla felt like she was coming out of a trance.

Ya-nhar-aswad! Janey Mack.

Holy Mary Mother of Divine Grace.

Her mind raced. What had she done?

Peter's crumpled body lay on the pavement in front of her. Looking back up, she noticed that his older brother was gone. But moments later, he reappeared, with an adult in tow.

'That's her!' Peter's brother said, pointing at Layla. 'She's the one who picked a fight with Peter!' With a sinking feeling, Layla realized who this man was – the Chair of the Board. Mr Cox. He was the one person who had not wanted Layla to join the school, but the principal had overruled him.

Things were about to get very interesting.

Chapter 5

The couch was very comfortable. *Too* comfortable. Layla knew that she was in trouble, but she could happily sit on this sofa all day, the cushions a cool cocoon. She was in the waiting room outside the principal's office, which was in the main reception building she had come into only this morning.

What a wild first day.

The carpet in the room was dark blue and lush, and a low wooden oval table sat in front of Layla, displaying assorted magazines and an enormous bunch of flowers in the middle. The vase holding the flowers was beautiful, slender and shapely. The blues and greens of the glass reminded Layla of the ocean, matching the gentle quiet in the room. Soft light filtered in through the one window to her left. A large painting of the shore hung above Layla's head, and above the squat bookshelf hung a noticeboard with posters on all sorts of exciting activities: a robotics competition, classes for rowing, skiing, maths. Layla thought they looked interesting, but realized she might not last long enough at the school to get to try any of them.

She sank further into the deep black leather seat, stroking the smooth texture of the arm and wished the couch would swallow her up so she wouldn't have to deal with this whole mess.

What came over me?

She racked her brain to try to understand what had been going through her mind when she decided to deck Peter, but all she could remember was being told she wasn't Australian, being shoved to the ground and then seeing red. She hated it when people said that. And then when she went back to Sudan they said she wasn't Sudanese either. Layla furrowed her brows angrily.

KMN. Like, who am I then? Who is Peter to tell me that I'm not AUSTRALIAN!

Layla's fists balled up with anger as she started to get wound up again. It was just so unfair. People yelled similar stuff to her family on the street too, though Mama usually laughed in their faces. Why did people care so much about it anyway?!

Gosh, I wish Dina was here – she'd get it. Oh, and what I'd like to say to that –

'Layla?'

Uh-oh. Layla's train of thought was interrupted, and she was rudely returned to reality. Her mum and dad had just walked into the waiting room. She was angry at Peter, but it was Mama and Baba she was really worried about! The look on their faces as they entered the ornate room did not bode well. The twins bounded in behind her parents, their loud voices quietening as soon as they entered the room. Even they knew this wasn't a place or time for celebration.

'*3amalti shnu ya bit?!*' Baba's steely soft voice asked Layla what she'd done. His voice might have been low, but Layla could hear the danger and disappointment in his tone.

Her stomach twisted and she lowered her face, unable to meet her father's eyes. Both parents stood in front of Layla on the sofa, clearly not interested in sitting. The twins had different ideas, jumping on to the couch next to Layla.

'Wow, this is so comfy!' Sami squealed, momentarily forgetting the gravity of the moment.

'*Shhhhh!*' everyone whispered sharply at the same time, and Sami snapped his hand up to cover his mouth and muffle the laugh that immediately followed.

This is going to be majorly *awkward.*

The meeting with the principal was short. Peter and his brother had reported that Layla picked a fight with Peter for no reason and attacked him at the school gate. As such, Layla would be suspended, put on probation and her scholarship was no longer guaranteed. For Layla to come off probation and renew her scholarship, not only would she need an excellent academic year, the principal said, but she needed to go above and beyond to prove that she wanted to be at this school and that she was committed to learning, inclusion and mutual respect. Mr Savage had been kind, but firm in his disappointment and decision.

What the actual fotonias! This was unbelievable! Peter and his brother had lied! Not only had they insulted her and pushed her to the ground, but they couldn't even admit it? And they walked away without even a scratch! Despite the fact that she'd headbutted Peter, of course.

Layla's jaw had been clenched and her teeth had ground together as the principal talked, her reputation being dragged through the mud in front of her eyes. Mr Savage hadn't even asked her what had happened. This was soooo unfair.

Layla opened her mouth to interrupt the principal and correct the record, but her mother had other ideas. Layla felt a strong, sharp squeeze on her upper arm. *OUCH!* Looking round, Layla saw her mother giving her the scariest side-eye she'd ever seen. *Don't even dare talk,* that look said. Layla shot back a message with a glare: *WHAAAAT! For the Love of Allllllllahhhhhhh!* She couldn't disobey such an obvious instruction though – Sudanese culture was all about respecting and listening to your elders, particularly in situations like this. So she stayed silent – furious, fuming and frightened.

The car ride home was even more excruciating. As soon as they buckled their seatbelts, Baba met her eyes in the rearview mirror. 'We will talk about this *fi-alʒasha*,' he said, meaning that this would be discussed at dinner, like all important family affairs.

That was that.

Layla felt that if she opened her mouth, she would either start screaming or crying, or both. Neither option would help, so she did nothing at all. The twins, in an attempt to cheer her up, told a couple of her favourite lame jokes, but nothing worked. Her arm throbbed where Mama had squeezed her earlier.

Layla peered over the back of the driver's seat, trying to see her parents' faces. *Nothing!* The two were sitting in silence, both looking straight ahead. Her parents usually talked about work or listened to the news on the local ABC radio station. Not today. It was like they were going to a funeral. Mama, in the

70

passenger seat, sat with an inscrutable look on her face, hands folded in her lap and resting on the sparkling material of the *toub* she wore. It must have been an important day at work, as she was wearing one of her fanciest *toubs*, the traditional married Sudanese woman's outfit. After about ten minutes, she pulled out her iPad and began answering some emails.

Baba, driving, gripped the steering wheel tighter than usual – his knuckles white. But that was the only indication that Baba was frustrated, aside from the distinct lack of any conversation.

Even the twins were at a loss. Sami, sitting next to Layla, looked at her forlornly, and took her hands in his. His baby face looked up at his big sister, brown eyes wide and hopeful.

'It'll be OK, Layla,' he whispered reassuringly.

Layla nodded, her stomach feeling sick for the second time that day.

At dinner, she finally got her chance to speak. After everyone had been served the main – *cosa bi-al-bashamel*, a courgette béchamel dish that Mama loved but Layla hated – Mama put her utensils down and looked at Layla.

'So, what happened, *Min razyatik?*' said Mama, asking Layla to explain the incident from her point of view.

Layla regaled the family with the story – the pushes by Peter, the insults, being told to go back to where she came from, calling him a convict, headbutting him. Halfway through, the tears that had been threatening since the car ride home started to overflow.

'I know I did the wrong thing, Ma,' she choked after finishing the story, wiping snot from under her nose. 'I know I shouldn't have snapped, or called him names, or been violent. I know you think that we should always be the better ones in a situation, like the Prophet Sallah-Allahu-3lahi-Wasalam always was. But Peter was so awful, and no one was telling him to stop or helping . . .'

Layla's body heaved with sobs, heavier now. She didn't know what was going on, or how to handle this kind of thing. No one had said anything like this at ISB. There, everyone had been different. People might have been mean, but they never told her to leave the school. Or the country. Why were they so cruel at this fancy school where people were supposed to be smarter, richer and better together? Better together, that was pretty much the school's motto!

'Do you know who those boys are, Layla?' Baba asked.

Layla shook her head. What did he mean?

'Peter and his older brother, Jack – they are the Chair of the Board's sons. They are a powerful family at the school, *habibti*.'

Oh dear. She really couldn't have picked worse enemies.

'So, wha-wha-what are you saying?' Layla asked between sobs. 'That I shouldn't have done anything?'

'Well, you know we don't ever agree with fighting. We're very disappointed when any of our children fight with their fists – or, in your case, your head! Calling someone names is never acceptable – it makes us no better than the people we're fighting, and it's not very Islamic. But it does sound like you were physical in self-defence, not an attack like the other boys said. Is that right?' Mama asked.

Layla nodded slowly, her braids barely moving. 'OK then. You were protecting yourself. That's all right, *habibti*.' Mama reached over to wipe a tear off Layla's face, her own face soft. 'That's OK. We all need to protect ourselves sometimes.'

'But now what do we do?' came Layla's sniffling response.

'Well, at the moment, it's your word against theirs, no?' Baba said. 'And the principal hasn't even asked you for your side of the story, really. What about the other kids who were there? Have any of them talked to the principal?'

Layla shook her head vigorously, and still her braids didn't move much.

'Maybe if you get someone to report what *really* happened, or maybe share one of those videos that you said were recorded, you can get the suspension overruled. Do you want us to have a chat with the school?'

Layla looked up to the corner of the room and pursed her lips, salty tears dripping down her chin. 'I don't know, Mama. I don't want to make it any worse.

What do you think, Ozzie?' She wasn't super close to her older brother, but she really respected his opinion.

Ozzie shrugged. 'Getting parents involved always makes things messy, I reckon,' he said, licking the last bits of sauce off his fingers. 'I'd stay low key, but that's just me.'

'Maybe we leave it for now, then,' Layla said, looking to her parents. Low key might be the best key.

'OK, *habibti*, if that's what you really want. We can stay out of it. But the moment you want backup, we're here for you. Nobody messes with the Husseins.'

Her parents discussed the fact that while she was on suspension she could focus on study, maybe ask the teacher for extra credit work like she used to do in primary school. Suddenly Layla remembered the other thing that had happened that day – she'd been thrown out of class by her homeroom teacher too! Layla dropped her face into her hands. Her parents hadn't heard about that yet, but they were probably not going to be as forgiving about *that* incident.

What a mess! What a hot, hot mess.

Chapter 6

Layla lay on her bed that night, texting Dina. Layla shared the big bedroom with the twins; she had the top bunk and the twins slept on the double bunk bed at the bottom. The room was a mix of her stuff and theirs: posters of SpongeBob SquarePants (theirs) alongside posters of a giant mystical tree (hers) and Muhammad Ali (hers *and* theirs). Both their sets of drawers were equally messy, with piles of books, toys and jewellery pieces strewn across the tops of the dressers and all over the floor. Layla liked to think it was an organized mess, but her parents never seemed convinced.

Dina knew Layla inside out. Back at ISB, they had spent every minute together: they sat next to each other in class, hung out with each other at lunchtimes and would even do after-school activities together. Layla missed Dina sooooo much, especially today. Her friend had been super supportive when Layla first got the scholarship, but as the first day of school got nearer they both began to realize how much things would change. School was not going to be quite the same. Gosh, how Layla wished Dina was with her now though. She always knew what to do.

Layla: *Dina I had da WORST day.*

Dina: *OMG what happened?*

Layla: *This guy fully yelled terrorist stuff at me in front of the whole school! I totes went ape at him hey. lol. I ended up HEADBUTTING HIM.*

Dina: *OMG YOU DID WOT?*

Layla: *Ikr. It was lit but obvs I got in maaaaaajor trbl.*

Dina: *??*

Layla: *Suspended yo.* ☹

Dina: *U GOT SUSPENDED? U?*
Layla? DUDE!

Layla: ** 😔 **

Layla threw her phone across the bed, overcome by a sudden wave of sadness. Only a few hours ago she had been so positive about this new school and the adventures ahead, but now she didn't know what her future would be. She wasn't the kind of girl who got mixed up in fights or suspended. She had known people like that, but that wasn't her. She knew who she was – she was smart, loud and a bit of a joker. She was always being told off by teachers for being noisy and disruptive, though she never got into *real* trouble. Now, with all this, in one day, had MMGS turned her into someone else? How had that even happened? It was so unfair! OK, she shouldn't have tried to make the other kids laugh at Ms Taylor, but Peter and his brother were *so awful*! How was it that they could get away with treating people like that?

She had to do something to make this right.

Layla thought about the people she looked up to. Mama and Baba often talked about those throughout history who had fought for justice to make the world a better place. People like the Prophet Mohammed (Peace and Blessings be upon Him), Nelson Mandela, Maya Angelou. She wondered how they would fight back against the lies Layla was dealing with. It was kinda wild. They all were strong, powerful people, but they didn't take revenge on those who hurt them. *Rah* . . . She hadn't realized that before. How on earth were they able to be respectful to people who were so awful to them?

Layla recalled a story Mama had told her about the Prophet Mohammed (PBuH) where he would walk past an old lady's house daily on his way to the mosque. This old lady hated him so much that she would throw her rubbish at him, every time without fail. The Prophet never responded to her, but would just pass by silently.

One day, she wasn't there to throw anything at him. Her absence noted, *Rasoul* (another name for the Prophet) made some inquiries and her neighbour informed him that she was in bed sick. Later that day, the Prophet went to visit the woman – not to take revenge on her when she was weak, but to look after her and pay his respects. The woman was so impressed by the Prophet's actions and kindness of character that she eventually became Muslim.

Layla sighed, thinking of this tale. It was a pretty good story, but she wasn't as kind as the Prophet! I mean, he was a *prophet*! Sure, all her other role models had also encouraged their followers to be non-violent or forgiving, but they also stood up for what was right.

So what am I supposed to do in this situation, yo?!

Layla took a deep breath. Her head hurt. It was all a bit much really. She could feel her forehead throbbing and turned to look at herself in the mirror. *AH!* There was a great big bruise on her forehead where she had headbutted Peter! Yow! Maybe it was a good thing that she wasn't going to school tomorrow after all.

Sami and Yousif bounded into the room, followed by Ozzie, who lazily sauntered behind. The twins jumped on to their bed and Ozzie leaned inside the doorframe. Layla sat up and swung round, her legs hanging off the side of the top bunk bed.

'So, about what happened,' Ozzie drawled, looking down on his phone and flicking through Instagram before glancing at Layla.

'Yeah . . .' Layla's voice was quiet. Ozzie was sometimes a bit mean to her, but she looked up to her big brother and wanted him to like her. He was, like, the dopest person she knew. He wore cool clothes, was smart enough to get good grades (but never seemed to need to study) and was also super athletic (he won all the sprint races at school). His friends were always coming through the house calling Mama 'Aunty' and, although they never really paid Layla much attention, she wished she could hang out with them, cruising around the suburb on skateboards and BMX bikes. They were always getting up to some adventure. Ozzie mostly ignored her, but moments like these, when he actually wanted to talk to her, always made her feel special.

'You OK?'

Layla met her brother's eyes.

'What do I do, Ozzie? I know you said not to involve Ma and Ba.' She looked down again, legs swinging. 'And it's not like I'm scared of Peter, but, I mean, what if he or his brother hurts me next time? I don't have anyone to back me up. It's not like ISB where I've known everyone for years and they all know me.'

'They're bullies. You just have to be smarter than them. You're a clever kid, so work out how to outsmart them rather than outfight them.'

With that, Ozzie turned round and left, putting his ear to his phone. 'Oiii, cuzzzz!' His voice trailed off as he walked down the hallway.

Layla rolled her eyes and then turned over on to her stomach, pushing herself off the bed and hopping on to the twins' bed below. They had been sitting quietly and watching the conversation.

'What do you boys think, hmm? What should Sister Layla do?'

Sami and Yousif started bouncing on the bed, one up, the other down. 'Let's play Lego! *Yeh!* Let's build something! Maybe that'll fix it?'

Layla laughed. What a time. She'd been thrown out of class, headbutted the chairman's son, been suspended from school and possibly lost a scholarship. She highly doubted Lego was going to fix *this* particular situation, but maybe it would help take her mind off things.

The twins scrambled off the bed, grabbing their stash of Lego from the dresser, grinning and babbling between themselves. They loved Lego and had requested a box of it for both Eids every year. As Layla poured the blocks on to the rug on the floor, her mind wandered, and she remembered one of the posters she had seen on the noticeboard in the principal's office. Maybe she could build her way out of this one after all. Maybe there was a path to saving the scholarship that she'd worked so hard for, which got her one step closer to her dream of being a world-famous bejewelling adventurer.

Layla was suspended, so she wasn't supposed to go to school all week. But she needed to talk to Mr Gilvarry about her idea. That evening, she worked with her mother to carefully word an email to the year coordinator, who gave her permission to visit the tech building to fetch the notebook that she'd pretended she'd left behind.

The next day, Layla convinced her dad to take her back to school before they picked up her brothers. It had been less than 24 hours since everything happened, but that didn't dampen Layla's mood when she walked into the woodwork room on Tuesday afternoon.

'Mr Gilvarry!' Layla strode confidently into the tech room, pausing at the door to breathe in the smell of pine and varnish.

'Layla!' The teacher looked up from the bench where he sat on a stool, sanding away at a wooden carving in front of him. He placed the carving carefully down on the tabletop and roughly brushed the sawdust off his dirty maroon apron. 'What can I do for you? I thought you weren't coming into school all week?'

'Yes, yes, I'm still on suspension, but I'm a hustler, ya know?' Layla chuckled to herself as she channelled her inner grifter. *Focus, girl! All right. You got this.* Layla took a deep breath and unloaded.

'Listen, Mr Gilvarry, I've got something very important . . . and I think it could change things . . . but I think . . . well, I don't really know what I'm doing so I might need, like, your help,' Layla stuttered, the words spluttering out quicker than she could move her mouth.

'Slow down, Layla. What's going on?'

Layla took a deep breath, focusing on her tech teacher's jolly face. 'Well, I saw there was a competition, a robotics competition, and I wondered if you knew anything about it because, well, I want to enter.'

Mr Gilvarry's face broke into a grin. 'Oh, of course! The Grand Designs Tourismo – GDT – is a huge deal!'

Layla soon learned that the GDT was the biggest robotics-invention competition in the country, and the top three ideas in each state would go on to compete in the national finals. The winner of the national final featured in a half-hour show made by the ABC, and that wasn't even the *most* exciting part.

Mr Gilvarry went on to explain: 'The team that wins the nationals goes to the international final in Germany. It's a *huge* thing, and MMGS always does really well. In fact, the current board chairman, Mr Cox, was part of a team that competed in the international final years ago! They almost won, but the competition was stopped because the Berlin Wall was coming down. Big year, that was – for Germany and for MMGS.' Mr Gilvarry chuckled under his breath.

OMG. This is perfect. If she was part of a winning team, the principal would definitely be impressed enough to drop the probation and maybe even renew her scholarship. This was for sure her way back in. She needed the scholarship to stay in this school. MMGS was the only way Layla could see her dream of being a world-class adventurer become reality. This school held the key to her future. She couldn't let that slip out of her fingers now.

The only problem was, she had no idea how to invent anything. She could build stuff, sure. But that's not quite the same thing as *inventing* . . .

'How do I join a team, Mr Gilvarry? I want to be a part of this; it sounds epic!'

'Well, I'm the teacher looking after the competition, so I know all the groups entering. Our strongest team is run by one of your classmates, actually. They've been working together since last year. I am not sure if you know him – Peter Cox?'

Layla's heart sank like a heavy stone in the front lake of the school.

No, no, no. Not Peter! How did this boy end up ruining everything all the time?

Layla swallowed, her mouth suddenly dry. 'Yeah, I know Peter. Um, is there any other team you recommend joining though?'

My Gilvarry's eyes went to the ceiling as he searched his brain. 'Hmm,' he grunted. 'Let me think. The Sasquatches are a good group, but never seem to get anything finished on time, the Hilarions are our all-female team . . .'

The tech teacher listed a bunch of other names, but none inspired much confidence. It appeared that Peter's group was clearly the one most likely to take out the competition. Apparently, Peter's dad had been training him up for this his whole life, buying him robotics sets as soon as he turned three. They were Mr Gilvarry's favourite team too. But Layla could not bring herself to work with the very person responsible for getting her suspended.

'Mr Gilvarry,' she said, an idea popping into her head like an environmentally sustainable fluorescent light bulb. 'Can I just start my own team?'

'Oh yes, well, I suppose you could. I don't usually recommend that newcomers or even new arrivals –'

'You mean new arrivals like new to the school? Cos I've been in Australia pretty much my whole life, you know . . .' Layla interrupted. She trailed off, realizing that she didn't really know who she was talking to. Maybe Mr Gilvarry would get angry? *What's wrong with me? Why am I so touchy about stuff right now?*

'Ah, yes,' Gilvarry continued, barely skipping a beat, 'new arrivals to the school. But anyway, look, I don't usually encourage people to enter on their own, but I understand it might be difficult for you to simply slip into a team when they've been working on their projects for months now. So, if you really want, you can be in a team of one.'

Layla's imagination filled with all the things she could work on. How hard could it be?

'Do you know much about inventing things?' Mr Gilvarry's voice interrupted her train of thought.

'No, but I can learn and learn quickly! I'm really great at fixing things and I'm always keen to know how things work.'

The teacher nodded, his great belly jiggling in time.

'All righty then. I guess I can start you off with some reading, some stuff online and in books. And then we can brainstorm some ideas?'

The teacher walked to the back of the class and into a corner so shrouded in darkness that Layla hadn't even noticed it was there. He came back with a high stack of books that reached Layla's nose when he handed them to her.

'You should really buy a Kindle,' Layla said, her legs almost buckling under the weight and her arms feeling like they were about to be ripped out at the shoulder sockets. 'Or any kind of e-reader. These books are heavy and dusty and –' Layla sniffed – 'they smell. What is that, mould?'

Mr Gilvarry laughed. 'Oh no, no. You can't buy these books online. That's the best part of it. If you want to invent something nobody has thought of before, you need to read the things that others don't read, look in the spaces other people are not looking in. That way, you can bring inspiration from all over the place into your work. And these books are a great place to start.'

Layla craned her neck round the stack of books in her arms. Indeed, the books were not all about how to become a carpenter or robotics designer or engineer. There were stories on building new worlds, on discovering new species, on science and art and philosophy. Layla wasn't sure she was going to get through all of these. In fact, she was *certain* she wasn't going to get through all of them. But she would definitely be giving it a red-hot go! *Rah*, this was cool. Mr Gilvarry was like her very own Mr Miyagi from *The Karate Kid*. Yes! She'd always wanted a powerful magic mentor. Maybe Gilvarry wasn't magic, but with bus-driver socks like his, anything was possible.

'All right then, sir. Thanks so much. I'll read these over my next few days at home and come back to you next week with some ideas. Sound good?'

'Yep. Next time you come through, remind me to give you the paperwork for registration. Now head along and HAVE FUN!'

Layla wobbled outside with the stack of books, unable to see what was in front of her. A few steps out of the building, she bumped into someone, making a loud *thud* and almost knocking them both over. The voice on the other side of the book stack was hard and unmistakable.

'Watch it, you black dog!'

It was the voice that had snarled at her only yesterday. Clenching her teeth and closing her eyes to stop the hot, furious tears from spilling over, Layla opened her mouth to retaliate, but nothing came out. Her mind went blank.

What — what — why can't I say anything? What's happened to my voice? Layla's heart was beating a mile a minute, and she noticed that she was trembling. She wondered if this was how Mama and Baba and Ozzie felt when people said stuff or yelled at them in the street. They didn't talk much about the incidents where people were racist or Islamophobic, but Layla had heard her parents talk to Ozzie about what to do in the case of verbal or physical abuse. She couldn't believe that her fast-talking tongue had betrayed her when she needed it most. It was like her brain had just run away. *C'mon, c'mon!*

Layla's eyes flew open.

Peter was gone. There was no one in sight, and she was standing alone in front of the building. She could have almost sworn she had imagined his words, had it not been for the tears running freely down her cheeks. She couldn't wipe them without putting the books down. '*Ya Allah*, give me strength!' she whispered under her breath. Her emotions were a mix of terror and deep, dark anger. Oh, how she would show that Peter Cox that he had messed with the wrong girl. Oh, she would make him pay by taking the thing she now knew he wanted – the GDT prize.

Watch me invent the best thing since fried cauliflower!

Chapter 7

Layla spent the rest of the week with Baba at home. He had reorganized his shifts at the hospital, where he worked as a medical technician, so he could be at home with his daughter.

It'll be a nice, relaxing week and I can probably sleep in for another hour, then maybe have breakfast and read a book until lunch. Layla was lying in bed, staring up at her cream bedroom ceiling, lips pursed as she hummed. Layla loved looking at the ceiling and making plans, it was her morning routine before she got out of bed. *Maybe I can have an afternoon nap before everyone else gets home too.* She smiled to herself and snuggled into her favourite sleeping position: on her side, knees up to her chest, right cheek resting on top of her right palm. But Layla's rest was short-lived. Baba clearly had other ideas.

Later that day, Layla sat curled up on the lounge-room couch in a blue *jalabeeya*, reading a book by Isaac Asimov. Her braids were up in a loose knot, spilling over her shoulders. Baba walked towards Layla with purpose, her father's distinct gait an obvious sign that she was just about to be given a chore. *Oh no!* Layla squinted and pretended to be concentrating *really hard* on the book so that maybe he wouldn't disturb her.

Kareem was in his corduroy work pants and a polo shirt that he'd bought from Kmart when they first moved to Australia. 'I still fit!' Kareem would tell Fadia proudly every time he wore it. Fadia was less than impressed, as the light blue material was worn through and there were holes in the seams. She had patched the sleeves up so many times the shirt made him look like a pirate. Today, though, Kareem wasn't in the mood to boast about his shirt.

'You're being punished! This is not a holiday, *ya bit*!' Baba admonished Layla, whose nose was almost touching the page of the science fiction novel Mr Gilvarry had lent her. 'Layla, bringing the book closer to your face won't convince me to change my mind.'

Layla glared at her father over the pages, annoyed.

'Stop with that face! I took a whole week off from day shifts to take care of you after that incident with Peter, so –' Baba noticed the book Layla was reading. 'Wait a minute! Asimov? Where did you get that?'

Layla smiled to herself. Maybe this could work after all.

'Oh, Mr Gilvarry gave it to me. He told me to read a bunch of different things, so I can get original ideas if I want to invent something for the competition I told you about yesterday.'

Baba nodded, distracted. Layla knew that Asimov was one of her father's favourite authors, but Kareem read all his books in Arabic. Layla's father was always pronouncing names of authors and characters with a thick Arabic accent – in this case, 'Isaac Asimov' was said 'E-zayk Azee-moof'. Any time Kareem recommended a book or author to Layla, she had to figure out what the 'Aussie' pronunciation was before she tried searching online or in the local library.

Despite being impressed, Baba was *not* going to be distracted from his mission to get Layla off the couch. 'Well,' he said, standing at the foot of the cream leather couch, hands tapping on the furniture's shapely wooden arms. 'Even though this is a great book, and the movie is halfway decent too, you are going to spend the day helping me out in the garden, OK?' Baba tapped the top of the book pile that sat on the little table next to the couch. 'Also, where did these all come from? Are they from your teacher as well?'

The pile was high, and the books were still covered in a thin film of dust. Layla had dumped them hastily on the table, crowding out the numerous framed family photos on display. She even had to move the ebony statues that usually sat proudly around the photos to a different table – in fact, she'd hidden them in the drawers underneath the TV! Layla was hoping her father wouldn't notice that the large elephant and gazelle statues were missing. They were his favourite pieces of art, purchased from an old uncle who sold his wares on the edge of the Nile back in Sudan. Today, though, Kareem's mind clearly wasn't on his Sudanese home. It was, very firmly, on the weeding situation in his Australian backyard.

'*Yallah!*' Baba called, as he walked away from the couch towards the back door, his *shibshib* making a distinctive slapping sound against the tiles as he walked. 'I'm waiting!'

Grumbling, but relieved her father hadn't noticed the missing carvings, Layla put down the book and headed to the backyard.

Janey Mack! This was going to be a much more tiring week than she expected.

That afternoon, Layla heard her phone ping. She was outside at the time, on her hands and knees, brown fingers blistering from prying out weeds from the cracks in the concrete patio. The Husseins' backyard was very typically Queensland: the back door opened out to a concrete courtyard, which spilled out on to a square of grass the size of the family's lounge room. Garden beds bordered the grassed section, containing thick shrubbery: trees, which Kareem had painstakingly planted and watered regularly, and other random greenery that wouldn't stop growing, no matter how hard they tried. Layla had been tasked with pulling out the weeds in the concrete area first, then moving on to the weeds in the garden beds. But the moment she heard the familiar *ding* of her phone, telling her she'd got a Snapchat DM, her head snapped up and she scrambled up off the ground, bolting into the house.

Her phone was plugged in to the charger on the kitchen bench, the long iPhone cord grey from use. Pulling the cord out, Layla fumbled with the phone, stabbing her passcode in and smearing dirt all over the cracked screen. The phone buzzed as she entered her six-digit code (Baba was weirdly paranoid about Sudanese government interference, so they had to use long codes) wrong three times in her haste. *Calm down already!* Layla scolded herself. She took a deep breath and finally got into her phone. The notification was from Ethan. Layla's heart started beating a little faster. She hadn't thought she would hear from Ethan or Seb at all. How had they even found her on Snap?

> **Ethan:** *Hey, teach wanted me to tell you about some homework we have to do for next week. Email?*

Layla sighed. Ethan was just messaging to tell her about work, not to see how she was going.

> **Layla:** *Hey. It's LaylaTheWarrior@ gmail.com*
> **Ethan:** *Lol. The Warrior?*
> **Layla:** *Yeh, didn't you hear how I took Peter out, m8? Defs a warrior*

Layla scrunched up her nose. She knew she was trying to impress Ethan with this warrior chat, so was it a bit too much? Gah!

| Ethan: | *Yeh, that was wild. I saw the video on Leesa's snaps.* |
| Layla: | *Lol. So, like, what's his deal? Why does he hate me?* |

It was a few minutes before Ethan's reply came through, and Layla could have sworn she held her breath the whole time. Had she come across too strong?

Ethan:	*Peter's mean to everyone. Lol.*
Layla:	*Has anyone tried to stand up to him before?*
Ethan:	*Nah, no one wants to get into trouble . . . you know, with his dad and all.*

Layla sighed again. If no one else had been game enough to pick a fight with Peter, what was she thinking? *I suppose I wasn't really thinking at all.*

| Layla: | *Lol. True. I guess I'm just lyk dat.* |

Ethan:	*It was lit. U r defs a warrior.*
	[GIF]
Layla:	*[GIF] Wyd tonight?*
Ethan:	*Yo, my parents are actually*
	here tonight so we're having
	dinner together.
Layla:	*Oh cool!*
Ethan:	*Yeh. TTYL bae.*

Wow. Layla put her phone down, beaming. Ethan thought she was lit! And he called her 'bae'. This was definitely progress. Now she couldn't wait for the week to be over.

Outside with Baba again the next day, sweat dripping down her braids and forehead, Layla was becoming seriously frustrated. The sun was shining harshly on her head and the ground was heating up, making everything deeply uncomfortable. Worse, and more urgently, she needed an idea for her robotics invention, and all this patio-weeding was just wasted time and energy. She was slowly losing patience with the weeds and yanking them out too quickly.

Her father crouched down next to her and started tsking.

'Layla! What are you doing? You need to get the roots too. That's the whole idea!' Kareem demonstrated, for the third time that week, how he wanted his daughter to pull out the green wisps of growth. 'See, like this!' Kareem offered a weed and root ensemble to his daughter, who glared at him before shaking her head. Laughing, Kareem threw the plant over his shoulder and on to the pile of weed corpses behind him.

Layla growled under her breath. Her hands were starting to bleed from grabbing and twisting so many small plants and her legs were sore from crouching down.

I wish we had something that could just weed this whole patio without me having to do this! Maybe something had already been invented?

'Baba, is there a machine that weeds patios for you?'

Kareem, still crouching, stopped mid pull and looked at his daughter, steadying himself with his other hand. He thought about it, eyebrows furrowing together, then looked back down at the concrete and finished pulling out the weed. 'Well, Layla *habibti*, why don't you go and find out? Maybe that's something you can try to design – it would certainly save people like me from having to hear grumbling when they ask their naughty daughters to help out!'

HA! This was an opportunity she couldn't miss. 'Oh, sweet! I'll just go do that now!'

Before Baba could even utter a word in response, Layla had run into the house, slamming the flywire door hard.

'*Barra7a*, Layla!' Baba yelled from outside.

Layla grinned. That door just couldn't handle the Layla flick, you know? Without even changing into her indoor *shibshib*, Layla ran into the bathroom.

Oh, thank goodness I got out of that!

Running her hands under the sink, the green stains and mud slowly came off her fingers, revealing puffy red blisters. Maybe the weeding experience would be worth it if it gave her an idea for her invention.

♡♡♡

Chapter 8

Layla spent hours on her laptop that afternoon, googling things like 'how to weed a patio properly' and 'machines that can help you prune your garden faster'. Although it didn't seem like there was the perfect product out there, it did seem like a complex issue. There were forums upon forums of people discussing the best technique to pull out a weed with its roots, what sort of weed poisons were the most effective, the best time of year to weed. So many details and so many opinions, Layla almost didn't know where to begin!

As Layla's eyes started to droop with exhaustion, the *Maghrib* prayer began pouring out of the speakers of Baba's computer behind her.

'Allahhhhhhhhh-hu-Akbar, Allaaaaahhhhh-hhhhhh-hu-Akbar!'

Layla jumped and looked around. Her hands had been resting on the keyboard, pressing down on a couple of keys. The laptop was angrily making *ping-ping-ping* noises. Layla sighed. Ah, if she was bored of this project already, how on earth was she going to be able to keep interested enough to actually invent something?

Layla shook her head and went to the bathroom to do *wudhu*, the ritual washing before you pray. Maybe she would feel a bit better after she had taken some time out to talk to Allah. It usually calmed her down a little bit. As she wiped her face with wet hands and ran cool water over her head, the back of her neck and tops of her ears, she felt herself relax. She never really liked doing *wudhu* – getting her braids wet was kind of annoying – but she often felt better afterwards. Mama said that doing *wudhu* helped wash the sins away. Who knew – but it definitely washed away the sweat from all the weeding!

After praying, the family sat down for dinner. Baba began his nightly routine of enquiring about how everyone's day had been. Strangely, Ozzie refused to engage when asked about his job hunt. 'Nobody wants to hire *me*!' he had snarled under his breath, and, unusually, Kareem dropped the topic. Layla felt for her brother; she'd seen him spend hours perfecting his résumé and walking around the shops handing them out, waiting for a phone call that never came.

Baba then turned to Layla and asked his daughter how her research for a robotics invention was coming along.

'Ah, it's harder than I thought it would be!' said Layla, slightly exasperated. 'I guess I don't know anything about weeding, so I don't know what's right and wrong?'

Baba nodded with understanding, his moustache covering the knowing twitch of his lips. 'Well, that's your first mistake then, Layla.'

Layla cocked her head. What was Baba talking about?

Kareem rubbed his hands together, the plate in front of him wiped clean from the evening's meal of *cosa bi-al-bashamel*. The oven tray with the courgette dish still sat steaming in the middle of the dinner table. They were getting through quite a bit of *cosa* this month. Baba leaned forward in his characteristic way, like he was about to tell Layla a secret.

'When you're trying to solve a problem, why solve someone else's, hmm?' he asked rhetorically. 'Why don't you invent something that would help *you*? That way, you already know all about the problem, and don't have to guess like with the weeding.' Baba leaned back, satisfied that he had dropped some liquid gold.

Layla's eyebrows furrowed because she thought she understood, but wasn't quite sure. Just before she could follow up with a question, Ozzie chimed in.

'Yeh, it happens all the time, right. People think they know what's good for us – like Muslim people – and come up with random ideas to fix us, without asking us what we actually want.' Ozzie looked at his sister intently. 'You know what I'm talking about!'

Layla looked down at her plate, the creamy sauce of the béchamel pooling around the mincemeat. She scratched the back of her neck, unsure. She didn't really know specifically what Ozzie was talking about, but maybe she kinda got it. Like, when she watched the news and the politicians were talking about African gangs. Everyone on the TV had an opinion on Africans, but nobody ever asked any other African people or the kids themselves why they didn't have a place to hang out or what they wanted to do.

Layla grimaced, annoyed.

Maybe she *did* know what Ozzie meant.

The twins piped up, interrupting Layla's train of thought. 'Yeh! Us too!' they said together. 'Nobody listens to what we want!'

Layla laughed to herself. Nobody did listen to the twins, but that was because they mostly wanted to eat chocolate and play in the park all day.

Mama reached over and started rubbing circles with the palm of her hand on Layla's back reassuringly. 'It's OK, *habibti*. You can't fix all the problems of the world. For now, the best thing for you to do is figure out what problem you want to attempt to fix and think of a solution for that,' Mama said.

A problem that she had that she could fix? Well, the only problem that she could think of right now was that she had to deal with bullies at school, but she couldn't build a robot to fix that. Or could she?

The rest of the week of suspension flew by in a blur of gardening, helping Baba with chores around the house, chatting with Dina and messaging Ethan. Dina seemed to be doing all right – actually, more than all right – at ISB without Layla. She'd become friends with a new girl who had joined her class, Bushra. Dina's feed was now full of Bushra and her doing all the things Layla and Dina used to do together: swapping lunches, sharing Tumblr posts and walking round the classroom block taking selfies. Layla didn't really know how to feel about it.

I mean, yeh, it's not like I wanted Dina to be alone, but she seems to have just replaced me with this other girl.

It probably didn't help that Bushra was super pretty too – she was Turkish, and the Turkish girls always looked so good in their unique hijab styles! Layla tried to convince herself that she wasn't jealous. After all,

Dina was still messaging her every day and spilling the ISB tea, but Layla couldn't help feeling a little bit sad that she was missing out on all the fun.

I guess I am kind of making new friends too, like Ethan . . .

Yeh, sure it was mostly about the homework, but Layla couldn't help it that every time a notification popped up with his name, her heart jumped a little. She pictured his secret smile, his curly red hair, the freckles on his nose . . . Oh dear. She definitely had a crush on Ethan. *Rahhhhh.* Liking Ethan was different from liking boys at the Islamic School too. At the Islamic School everyone was Muslim, so the idea of having a 'boyfriend' or 'girlfriend' wasn't really *allowed*, and although lots of the older kids had them anyway, everything happened on the DL. The students at MMGS weren't Muslim, so the rules were different, but they weren't Layla's rules. It wasn't like *she* wanted a boyfriend or anything . . . did she?

But it probably didn't even matter. Ethan wasn't the kind of boy who would fall for a girl like Layla anyway. This thought was in the bottom of her heart, so even though she got excited every time he messaged her, part of her knew that it was only ever going to be a fantasy. Cute white guys didn't like dark-skinned Muslim girls. That just wasn't how the world worked.

Layla made a mental note to ask Dina what to do when she saw her next. Dina knew how to handle situations like this. Despite the fact that neither of them had any romantic experience, Dina was definitely the one who seemed to be wiser in this arena. She just exuded worldly wisdom. And she was *beautiful*.

I wonder if she'll be at the mosque tonight?

It was Sunday, the last day of Layla's official suspension. She shot her bestie a message.

Layla:	*Hey, u@mosque tonight?*
Dina:	*Nah, I'm not praying atm.*
	Y, r u?
Layla:	*Me neither, bt wana talk2u.*
	Reckon u culd come thru
	anyway?
Dina:	**sigh* kkkkkk bt only cos*
	I <3 u!

Muslim women don't pray when they're on their period, and it was that time of the month for both of them, meaning they didn't need to go to mosque. But Layla didn't want to wait.

'BABA!' Layla yelled from her bedroom. 'Wait for me before you go to the mosque today!'

'*Tayyib yallah*, I'm leaving in five minutes!' her father bellowed back.

Layla jumped off the top bunk, quickly threw on her black abaya and hijab, and ran out of the room.

'Can we come too?' the twins yelled after her as she whisked past.

'If you are, come now!' she called, and laughed as she heard them falling over themselves to put on their *jalabeeyas* in time. They weren't even praying every day yet, but a trip to the mosque meant catching up with friends and a bit of fun, so they loved joining in.

At the mosque, Dina and Layla huddled together at the back of the women's section, bare-footed and cross-legged, whispering as the Imam led the prayer over the loudspeakers.

'Laylaaaa, what was so urgent? See, this is why you should be at ISB still. We wouldn't have to meet at the mosque like this if you were still at school! What's so special about this new place anyway? OMG come back, and then you can meet Bushra. She's new, from Turkey, she's really cool –'

'Oh, Dina, I don't wanna hear about *Bushra*.' Layla kissed her teeth, annoyed. This new girl was killing her vibe. 'Enough about what's-her-face –'

'Bushra!'

'Bush-whatever. Anyway –'

'Yo, you don't have to be so mean. You're the one who left me all alone at ISB.'

'All right, all right!' Layla's voice was getting louder, and someone shushed them. 'Listen. You know I'll always be here for you, D. You know that, right?'

Dina nodded her head in a circular way (*a little like a dolphin*, Layla thought). 'Yeh, I do know, Laylz, but I just miss you a lot. And I know you have these dreams of becoming, like, a world-famous adventurer, but I just wish you could do that and still stay at ISB.'

Sigh. This was a much longer conversation that wouldn't be solved now. 'I know you feel that way, D. But there's something more important that I wanted to talk to you about. It's a boyyyyyy . . .'

Dina's eyes lit up as Layla knew they would. 'OMG. TELL. ME. EVERYTHING!' Dina demanded, and Layla did.

As the prayers finished up and the aunties began chatting, Layla and Dina got to work. They whispered furiously, dissecting every conversation, every look, every Instagram post they could find, even his Tumblr account (they went in *deep*!).

It wasn't stalking – it was research.

'It's tricky, Laylz. Has he even had a girlfriend before? There are no pics of chicks. I can't even tell his type.' Dina sighed. 'He's cute and all, but you know how it is. He's not Muslim. I don't really know what to tell you.'

Layla did know. Marrying outside the Muslim community wasn't really a thing, and Layla had never heard of a Muslim having a boyfriend or girlfriend. The most she could do was have a crush on him and be satisfied with that.

'Sigh.' Layla said it instead of actually sighing. 'I guess you're right. I'll just enjoy his company, you know.'

Dina gave her best friend a side hug, and they leaned against each other and the wall of the mosque, legs outstretched in front of them, toes enjoying the cool air. As the congregation's chatter swirled around them, Layla breathed in deeply, resigning herself to the way things were.

Back at home, later that evening, Layla's phone pinged. It was Snapchat and a blurry photo of Ethan appeared.

You're coming back to school tomorrow, yeh? he asked.

Layla snapped a photo of her laptop back. *Yeh*, she wrote on the photo.

Excited? he shot back.

Layla snapped a photo of her face scrunched up and her tongue sticking out, then switched off the phone.

On one hand, she was excited to be going back to school. She was getting bored of being at home. She felt like her brain was dying a little bit when it wasn't working and learning new things – like her little grey cells were rotting away.

On the other hand, she wasn't looking forward to being in the same school grounds as Peter and his brother. A shiver ran through her as she thought about seeing the bully again, and her stomach clenched up.

Ya Allah, *help me handle this!* she silently prayed.

She couldn't afford to pick another fight with Peter – or anyone else – because her scholarship was already at risk, but she knew it was going to take all her strength to resist headbutting his smarmy face again.

Gah. Either way, Layla was nervous about going back tomorrow, perhaps even more nervous than she was on her first day of school. How were people going to treat her now? How was she supposed to act? Should she be all hard and smart-arse, or pretend that nothing happened and that all was cool? Maybe she should just lie low and try not to cause any fuss. That seemed sensible. Layla nodded to herself. *It's a shame I don't really have much of a track record in being sensible.*

Layla remembered one of her dad's favourite sayings: *al-baɡal bala kashal* . . . oh wait, no, that was a saying about onions. What was it again?

Oh yeh. *Al-jamel biyimshy, wa-al-kilab bitanba7.* The camel, or *jamel*, walks while the dogs keep barking. Baba had explained to her many times that if the camel has somewhere to go, then it doesn't get distracted by barking dogs as it walks past them.

Remember to be like the camel, Layla told herself. *Channel the* jamel *(hey, it rhymes!). Channel the* jamel. *You have places to be, gurl.*

And she drifted off to sleep, dreaming of camels, cool as custard, sauntering past packs of snarling, barking German shepherds.

Channel the *jamel* . . .

Chapter 9

The next morning, Layla repeated her new mantra as she prepared for her first day back at school.

Channel the jamel. *Focus on what you need to do, and don't pay attention to barking dogs.*

Layla hoped that if she repeated it enough times, it might sink in! In the car on the way to school, she stared out the window, muttering the mantra to herself. Her eyes moved rapidly left to right as she watched the world pass her by. As they dropped the twins and Ozzie off at ISB, Layla thought back to the days she'd spent at the small community school. How much simpler things had been then; it was chaotic, but it was like a second home.

Mama and Baba had tried to get her and Ozzie into other schools, but they had arrived in Australia in the middle of the year, so many schools weren't taking any new students, especially the ones that had a good reputation. The Husseins weren't here to play: they wanted their kids to get the best education possible, so they wanted them to go to the best school. Unfortunately, they lived too far away from many of the top-ranked schools to be in the 'catchment area'. Fadia and Kareem really tried. They had driven from school to school, Layla bopping up and down in the child seat in the back of their 1996 blue Toyota Corolla, next to Ozzie playing on his hand-me-down Nokia 3220 phone. At every school, her parents had tried to convince the principal to find space for their kids.

'Ozair and Layla are very smart,' they would explain. 'We've been teaching them at home. Both of them will slip right in and won't be behind at all.' They pleaded, but, alas, they had no luck at all. It didn't help that the pair looked so out of place on the Brisbane streets.

Fadia was in a *toub*, the traditional Sudanese dress, hands painted in black henna patterns and wrists dripping in the 23-carat gold bracelets that were gifts at her wedding. It is customary for Sudanese women to wear all their finery when out visiting or wanting to impress, so to wear all your gold and your best *toub* was normal for Fadia. But it was quite unusual for the Brisbane-born-and-bred men who were principals of these high-achieving public schools. The startled and bewildered looks she received as she sauntered into office after office never changed. Her tall black body would be loosely wrapped in a long red-and-gold sheet of cloth, sequins glinting and shimmering with every step. Fadia's *toub* of choice, that of a wealthy, educated mother, would have sent all the right signals to school principals in Sudan – here, it only sent messages of confusion.

It didn't help that Layla's father, in his crisp white *jalabeeya*, the traditional outfit of a Sudanese man, looked to the average Australian like he was wearing a loose white dress. The pair of them appeared to have been lifted straight out of the latest *National Geographic* magazine feature on Africa.

Was that racism? Mama thought so, and often talked about it at the dinner table. Baba's views were different. He said they'd been new arrivals so needed to fit in. It wasn't the white men's fault they didn't like the *jalabeeya*, and, since he was in their country, he would change his outfit to make them feel more comfortable. Kareem started wearing Western suits and very soon after found a job as a medical machinery technician.

Fadia never really adjusted to the Western way of dressing, and, although she settled in quite quickly at the public hospital as a doctor, she continued to keep up Sudanese appearances, reapplying henna every month and finding out about the latest *toub* fashion through her family WhatsApp group. 'These Australians need to know who we are and where we are from,' Mama would often say. After all, they were the ones who had hired her and begged her to move to this faraway continent. Fadia was a pretty good doctor, and Brisbane had a shortage of those, so the public hospital spent a long time convincing her to move with the family to the Land Down Under. If they wanted her here, Fadia would say, they would have to have her on her *own* terms. Also, all the doctors in Sudan wore a *toub*, so why couldn't she?

But aren't we also 'these Australians'? Layla would sometimes think, when Fadia went on one of her rants, although she'd never say it aloud. She didn't really know where she was from. Sudan? Brisbane? Australia? Sometimes she felt like she was so different she must really be from, like, Jupiter or something. She yearned for a time or place where she didn't have to question so much. But she wasn't sure that place existed, certainly not in Brisbane.

Luckily for Layla all those years ago, the last school that had been on her parents' list to visit was a small community school that had opened that year called the Islamic School of Brisbane. As soon as they pulled up in front of the school, hot and sweaty in that Toyota Corolla with no air conditioning, Fadia knew it was the right place. There were other parents in the car park, dropping their kids off at school, everyone wearing different types of clothing from around the world. There were outfits from India, Malaysia,

Indonesia, Fiji; parents from Egypt and Algeria, Nigeria and Serbia. Nobody stared at the two Sudanese parents who arrived with their afro-haired children skipping between them. Nobody questioned their presence as they walked up the cement path to the shipping container with the small billboard in front of it announcing OFFICE. Nobody asked Fadia and Kareem where they were from or asked them to repeat their names ten times. Here, they were people, just like everyone else. Here, their weirdness and difference were normal. Here, Fadia felt safe.

'We will bring them here,' she had said to Kareem, in a tone that indicated the decision was made. Fadia knew Kareem preferred the schools with white Australian kids because he wanted his kids to fit in and have a more 'Aussie' accent, but Fadia wasn't convinced it was a good idea. She didn't want Layla growing up among kids who would see her as different and would bully her because of it. She wanted her daughter to feel like she was safe and belonged. Fadia and Kareem came to a compromise – the kids would go to the Islamic School for primary, and they would reassess when they started secondary. *Inshallah*. Ultimately, Ozzie decided he wanted to stay at the ISB. Layla had thought she did, until she'd met Adam.

She blinked, then looked around, realizing they had reached the gates of MMGS. Baba was sitting in the driver's seat, scrolling through emails on his iPhone.

'*Aywa?* You're awake now?' he asked Layla, not looking up from the screen.

Layla scrambled, spluttering. How long had she been sitting there, just staring out the window?

'We've been here for over five minutes,' Baba explained, anticipating her question. 'You weren't responding to anything I was saying.'

Layla let out a squeak.

'AHH, sorry, Baba! I gotta go!' she called out as she wiggled her enormous backpack on and opened the car door. Her foot caught on her long skirt, and she tripped out of the car, falling forward, the momentum of her large backpack causing her to lose balance faster than she could accommodate. Her hands hit the concrete first, then her knees buckled, grazing on the concrete through her skirt. Layla looked up.

She was right at the front of the school, again, having hit the pavement.

Janey Mack! If only Dina was here.

Dina would have thrown out a hand to get Layla up off the ground, helped her dust her knees off and then cracked a joke, making them both laugh for days.

But Dina wasn't here, and Layla was — on hands and knees on the ground, students walking past, pointing, sniggering, snapping. Layla's maroon hijabied head fell, and she looked down at the concrete, taking a keen interest in the black spots of bubble gum that had yet to be pressure-washed off the path. What a way to come back to school. How was she always so clumsy? Could she never win?

Her eyes watered. Was it the fall, the embarrassment, or the angle of her head? Layla wasn't sure, but this was no time for scientific enquiry. Pushing herself up off her knees, she dusted the skirt down, turned round to close the car door (her father was talking on the phone now and had missed the whole thing!), straightened her shoulders and turned to walk through the gates of the school.

You got this, a voice piped up in her head. *You. Got. This. CHANNEL. THE.* JAMEL!

Whether the voice was real or not didn't matter. Layla smiled to herself, the smirk giving her a little extra pop in her step.

Yeh, she did. She GOT this.

Chapter 10

The rest of the morning passed without incident, and Layla started to relax. Seb and Ethan were being really nice to her and people had stopped staring at her as she walked past classrooms. The maths teacher seemed impressed by the effort Layla had put into the homework that Ethan had passed on. Layla might be a smart-arse, but at least she was still smart.

When the bell rang for morning tea, Layla's heart started to beat a little faster. Was she going to have to see Peter again? She shot Dina a quick Snap.

Layla:	*Deeeee, I'm worried about seeing Peter again. It's morning tea time.*
Dina:	*DW too much, Lay. Just channel your inner warrior. He's probs more scared of you than you are of him ha!*

Channel your inner warrior, Layla told herself as she packed up her books and followed the boys out. The warrior, the *jamel* – there was a lot to be channelling right now.

'You cool with hanging out with us today again, Laylz?' Seb asked. 'Don't worry about Peter, hey. He's a bit loose, but he won't do anything serious without his brother there.'

'Yeh, all right. I mean, are you guys cool with still being my mates? I mean, I am the new girl and, you know, after everything that happened with Peter, I don't want to get youse into trouble.'

'Nah, don't worry. You're cool to hang with us.'

Layla sighed with relief, then remembered to ask: 'Oh, BTW, did any of you have a copy of the video that Leesa took of the fight?' If Layla could get her hands on that video, maybe she could show the principal that Peter did push her and she wasn't the only one at fault.

'Nah, no idea, mate, sorry. Maybe ask some of the girls who take the bus? They might know her better. We don't hang out with girls, dunno if you noticed? Maybe you can be our token, and help us get in with the other girls in class, you know? Be our spy!'

Seb laughed, so Layla laughed along with them, though she noticed Ethan was quiet, facing away from the group and looking down. *Of course, they expect me to help chat to the other girls.* Layla sighed. If she was 'one of the boys', that came with the territory, she supposed. But did that mean she wasn't considered one of the girls worthy of being liked? Layla sighed again, and Ethan heard.

His eyes met hers, gently. His mouth twitched, like he wanted to say something, reassure her or something. But then Seb pushed him and made another joke. The moment passed. What had Ethan wanted to say?

Layla's heart hurt. Was this what it was like to grow up? Layla wasn't sure it was worth all the pain. *This struggle is so real . . .*

As they walked closer towards the group of boys, Layla switched her attention to searching for *that* face. The face that she remembered as twisted and angry. But it was nowhere to be seen. Where was he? A surge of adrenaline pumped through Layla's veins and she found herself hollering, 'Yo, where is Peter?' The boys started chuckling and jeering. 'Is he hiding? Is he too scared?' Layla didn't know where she was getting this bravado from, but acting bigger than she was, channelling her inner warrior, well, it was working! She felt strong. The cheering from the boys fed her and egged her on.

'Peter, where are youuuuuu?' she teased.

When she got to the group, the boys settled down a little.

Baz, the one who looked a little like Obama, jumped in. 'Nah, nah, don't get your knickers in a knot now. Peter is off sick today.'

Peter wasn't there. Oof! It was like a weight was lifted from Layla's shoulders, but she didn't change the expression on her face. She couldn't let them know how much easier she could now breathe.

'Not here!' She laughed and scoffed loudly. 'Ha! So, he really was too scared to see me, hey? Well, now we know who's reaaaaally the boss around here!'

Layla looked at the faces of the boys around her. She didn't know them well, but she didn't see hatred or anger; their faces were full of cheeky smiles and curiosity.

'Who?' Tony asked cheekily.

'Oh, mate. Me, of course!' Layla chuckled and pushed his shoulder good-naturedly. 'Now, you should all call me QUEEN!'

'Queen Layla does have a ring to it,' Seb mused.

Scotty rolled his eyes. 'You are wild. Peter is going to kiiiillllll ya!'

Layla smirked. 'He can try.'

The rest of the break flew by. Layla sat between Seb and Ethan, and as the laughs and jokes swirled around her, she realized that she might have made some new friends, but something still felt off. She was acting loud and brash, but that was only part of who she was. Would these boys still like her if they knew she was really a tree-climbing bejeweller, or that she went to mosque all the time, or that she had never been on a holiday? (Like, a *proper* holiday – trips back to Sudan didn't really count because visiting the family was WORK!) Her mother was always telling her that they weren't like other families. 'Just because other people do things doesn't mean we follow them mindlessly,' she would often scold Layla when Layla asked about sleepovers or expensive theme-park trips. 'We do what we think is important. Being different is the best way to be.' Layla wasn't convinced, but she never won that argument.

As she sat there, her mind distracted by these uneasy thoughts, she felt something on her arm. Annoyed, Layla absentmindedly tried to brush whatever it was away, and then jumped as she realized it was Ethan – poking her!

'Oi, Queen Laylz!' Ethan had been trying to get her attention. 'You coming to this party at the weekend?'

'Wait, huh? What are you talking about?'

The boys started laughing.

'You really went off into your own world there, didn't ya?' asked Tony. 'There's a big party at Baz's this weekend. His parents are away. All the cool kids are invited – you're in, right?'

Layla looked down at her fingers. 'Yeh, ha . . . totally,' she muttered, slightly under her breath. There was no way on earth her parents were going to let her go to a party that weekend. Not unless they had every single kid's parents over for tea to vet them first. Not only was there not enough time, Layla didn't know if she could handle the embarrassment . . .

'Lit! I'll send ya the deets. You're on Snapchat, yeh?' asked Tony.

'Yeh. Add me. QueenLayla . . .'

Layla's stomach dropped as she realized she was already lying to these boys, the people who were supposed to be her new friends. She felt bad, but it was too embarrassing to admit how different she really was to these kids. Hopefully they wouldn't figure anything out just yet.

The bell rang for the end of morning tea. She could deal with the party later . . . for now, she had to channel the *jamel*!

That afternoon they were studying history with Ms Taylor. Layla loved history but could never remember the specific dates of when different things happened. But Ms Taylor wasn't going to let her get away with anything this week.

'Layla, what do you know about Nelson Mandela?' Layla straightened up in her chair. This, she knew. 'They called him "Madiba", Miss,' Layla replied. 'He was this South African guy that went to jail for twenty-seven years because he was fighting against a-part-hide. Or maybe a-full-hide, something like that . . .' Layla smirked at her little pun. 'A-part-hide?' Ms Taylor laughed, humouring Layla.

'I think you mean "apartheid", but yes, that's who Nelson Mandela was. Do you know what apartheid was about, Layla?'

Layla wrinkled her nose. 'Wasn't it to do with something, like, white people being in control and not letting black people go to the same schools and stuff? I don't know the details, but my mum has a *huge* book on it.'

Ethan piped up next to her. 'Miss, wasn't it when the South African government separated the white people from the coloured people and black people because they thought white people were better?'

Ms Taylor nodded. 'Well done, Ethan. It was a pretty terrible and inhumane system.' The teacher turned round and switched on the projector, starting a documentary clip about the racist system that had governed South Africa for decades. As she explained what happened over nearly five decades, Layla felt her mouth becoming dry.

How did people find it within themselves to be so awful to each other?

As the class finished up and the students began packing their bags for home time, Layla walked up to Ms Taylor's desk. She was nervous, as they hadn't quite got off on the right foot on their first day, but something had been playing on Layla's mind.

'Hey, Miss.'

Ms Taylor looked up from her tablet, having presumably been checking the work they'd completed in class that day.

'Yes?' Her voice was neutral.

Better than icy, Layla thought. She must have been in an OK mood, so Layla went for it.

'How could something like that happen? How could people let that happen to other humans?' she asked.

Ms Taylor put her tablet on the desk, which was bare except for a single ceramic cup containing her tablet's stylus. *Hmm, bejewelling is definitely not her vibe.* Ms Taylor was a painstakingly neat and tidy individual. Her face betrayed little emotion as she carefully placed her hands on top of each other and looked up to Layla across her desk.

'Well, it is quite complicated. Why do *you* think?'

Layla involuntarily took a step back. She wasn't expecting to be asked her opinion. 'Maybe it had something to do with South Africa?'

The teacher shook her head and clasped her hands together, threading her fingers and then bringing them up to her chin. She leaned forward, her chin on her hands, her elbows on the table.

'But it's not just in South Africa. You know this happened in Australia as well?'

Layla slowly nodded her head. 'I mean, kinda. With Indigenous people?'

'Well,' Ms Taylor said, unthreading her fingers and shaking them out, then rubbing her hands on the tops of her thighs underneath the desk. Layla wondered why Ms T was moving about, agitated. She was usually so calm and collected.

Her hands stopped. 'Well. Yes. When the British first came to Australia, they did a similar thing to the Indigenous, or First Nations, people who lived here. The government were being bullies and using their power to make other people do what they wanted.'

Layla gulped. She had heard the details about how modern Australia came to be, but the idea that adults could be bullies, like a grown-up version of Peter, was terrifying.

'My grandmother was one of the people who suffered from their terrible policies. She was part of something called the Stolen Generation, when kids were taken from their mothers and put into missionaries. The government would then "own" them. It was a mess.'

Layla blinked furiously. She had no idea Ms Taylor had Indigenous ancestors. 'Oh . . . wow. Miss. Miss. Does that mean you're actually black too?'

Ms Taylor nodded. 'Yes, Layla. Even though I might not look it, I'm as black as they come. My people, the *Turrbal* people, are from around here.' The fine lines round Ms Taylor's mouth creased as she smiled, bittersweet.

'But that's not why I'm telling you this. Because around the world there are all sorts of people who have done terrible things. History is full of awful stories of war, hurt and anger.' The teacher took a deep breath. 'But you know what else we can learn from history? You know why I teach the story of Nelson Mandela, or Madiba, as we black mob call him too?'

Layla shook her head.

'Well, he's famous for his twenty-seven years in prison, yes. He's also famous for forgiving those who imprisoned him. He said that forgiveness liberates the soul and removes fear. He is a great example of how to move past the pain of someone who has hurt us, and work together. Although sometimes I wonder . . .' Her voice trailed off. Ms Taylor looked down at her desk, seemingly lost in thought, and a silence fell between them. The quiet grew louder, and Layla looked around her. The classroom had emptied out completely. All that was left were chairs and tables, slightly crooked and sitting askew. As the silence stretched, a slight discomfort crept over Layla. She cleared her throat.

Ms Taylor started, looking up at Layla like she was only just seeing her.

'Oh, Layla! You should head off now. Get home safely, dear.'

The teacher's fingers quickly flitted over the desk, picking up the tablet and plucking the stylus out of the ceramic cup. She turned to place them in the bag next to her feet.

Layla walked to her own bag, slipping her laptop into a pocket and slowly zipping up all the compartments. Ms Taylor's words rang in her head: *forgiveness liberates the soul*. It was easier said than done though. She walked from the classroom, waving a quick goodbye to Ms Taylor, and out to the front of the school.

Easier said than done. How did you forgive someone who was so awful to you? Who pushed you over and then lied about it? Who could ruin your future? A whole group of people who watched while you got yelled at, humiliated, bullied? Madiba had been in jail for decades. Maybe it gets easier to forgive as you get older. Or maybe he was just a better man. Layla shook her head slightly, trying to clear her thoughts. Her hijab rustled around her ears, having loosened while she was running around at lunch.

Nah, she wasn't going to forgive Peter. Not him. Never. She was going to find a way to beat him at the competition and show him, and everyone else, who was the boss. She had to win. She could forgive him after she'd beaten him.

Chapter 11

'Layla! Layla!'

Layla was standing in front of the school gate, waiting to be picked up. Her parents were late, as usual. In the background, she heard her name being called, the sound slightly muffled by the tunes blasting out of her white earbuds into her ears. Mama was always yelling at her to turn the volume down. 'You'll be deaf before you're twenty!' she would scold Layla, who would just poke her tongue out as a retort.

'Maybe that'll be good, so I won't have to listen to you!' Layla would reply.

Layla pressed Pause on the vintage iPod Nano, then pulled the right earbud out of her ear so it sat just below her earlobe, held to her jaw by the headscarf. The cheeky thing about wearing earphones with a hijab on was that no one knew you were wearing them. All the Lebanese girls at the Islamic School used to listen to music during school assemblies, their earphones hidden by their hijabs. You could always tell, though, if you looked closely – their fingers would be tapping along to a beat, even if their faces betrayed nothing.

'Lay-la!' the voice called again, but it wasn't the voice of one of her classmates, or even an awful Cox. It was the voice of Mr Gilvarry.

'Oh, hi, Mr Gilvarry! How are you doing?'

'Good, Layla, and you?'

'*Alhamdulillah*, I'm doing OK. I mean, I'm at school, and that's a start! Better than last week at least.'

Gilvarry chuckled. 'Yes, yes indeed. How are you going with those books I lent you?'

Layla groaned internally. The books! She had completely forgotten about them. She hadn't even finished the Asimov novel. They were sitting on her bedside table gathering dust – even *more* dust. She'd either have to fess up or lie to Mr Gilvarry. This thought made Layla remember the party Baba and Mama would never let her go to. Janey Mack, that party! She should probably tell Ethan. Layla quickly buried that thought. So much stuff to not think about.

Channel the jamel*!* she told herself, but that mantra wasn't for the purpose of avoiding responsibilities, though it would have to do for now.

Layla tuned back in to the conversation with her tech teacher. 'Oh, sir! I haven't had a chance to read them. In fact, my parents were so upset I was suspended that they made me do chores all week! They made me weed the patio.'

Gilvarry chuckled again. 'Oh, the excuses! It's OK, Layla, you don't have to make things up –'

Layla was slightly relieved Mr Gilvarry wasn't upset, but shocked that he didn't believe her. She jumped in. 'Oh, no, it's not an excuse, sir. I am serious.'

Layla stuck out her hands to show the teacher her blisters. She was usually quite self-conscious about her chubby hands and thick fingernails, which never looked anything like the hands of people on TV, but now wasn't the time to think about that.

'All right, all right,' he started to say, chuckling.

Layla was on a roll though and wasn't about to stop. She touched the tips of her fingers to each other to emphasize her next point.

'In fact, it was so much effort that I started researching whether or not there's a machine that could pull the weeds out, cos, if there isn't, I could maybe invent something that will fix the problem, you know?' Hands on hips, she took a deep breath and waited for her mentor's response.

Gilvarry stroked his beard with his right hand, beginning at his chin and slowly pulling down. Layla was shocked the entire beard could fit in his one hand, but when scrunched together it wasn't very much at all.

'Quite the beard, isn't it?' he said.

Layla nodded. 'Well, the first thing I'm thinking, young lady, is that you've got the right sort of perspective. Robotics should be used as something that fixes a problem needing to be fixed, not only something that would be "cool". Everyone usually tries to build something like a real-life Pokémon, but what use would that be?'

Layla could think of many uses for a real-life Pokémon. It could help her catch the other ones, for a start . . .

Gilvarry continued: 'My first thought was whether a robotics solution would be the best solution for the problem you've identified?'

Surely robotics was the correct solution for every problem. Baba was always talking about how in the future no one would have any jobs because machines would do everything. Except, of course, for the people who fixed the machines . . .

'What do you mean, sir?' she asked.

'Well, I have a weed problem in my backyard. They're shocking! They shoot up so very quickly and make my garden look like something out of the Forbidden Forest in Harry Potter.' Gilvarry's face gleamed in the afternoon sunlight as he smiled, his cheeks pink with sunburn and jolliness. 'But do you think I spend hours weeding every week?' he asked Layla, who shrugged, her eyebrows raised. Mr Gilvarry tugged on his beard. 'No, Layla, I don't. I use a spray on the weeds once a month. It kills the nasty little things down to the roots so they shrivel up, and all I do at the end of the weekend is sweep them up and throw them in the bin.'

Layla slumped, her school jacket stretching over her shoulders. 'Oh, so there is already a solution to the weeds issue.' She sighed, a long, deep sigh that betrayed the exhaustion of the last few days. 'God, why am I such a failure? I haven't even properly started this project and I'm already behind.'

This competition was her way of showing the principal and the chair that she deserved to keep her scholarship. It was also her way of showing that boy Peter who was boss. But, *ya-nhar-aswad*, her big project idea was already dead!

'Aye, there is one. But that doesn't mean you can't create another solution. Or, you can always think of another problem. Just because this one didn't work out doesn't mean you are a failure. It's just part of the process of learning. It would be too easy if everything worked out from the beginning, wouldn't it?' Gilvarry smiled at her again, then started, as if stung by a bee. 'Oh! What time is it? Oh dear.' Gilvarry looked down at his watch, then turned abruptly and started walking away, back up the path through the tall school gates. 'I've got to run now, Layla,' he called. 'But just remember – failures make the story more interesting!'

Layla waved at her tech teacher, his trademark bus-driver shorts and socks making him visible for miles. *How do those long socks never fall down?* she wondered, then turned back to look at the road, waiting for her ride.

There was almost no one left, as most people had been picked up already and the school buses had left a while ago. A couple of metres away, a few students from the year below stood huddled together, looking down at their phones. Layla sighed, looking forlornly at the iPod Nano in her hands, which only held 250 songs. The metal case of the Nano was scratched and weathered, and only a slight hint of the original rose-gold colour tint was visible. Layla ran her fingers over the little device, feeling the dents made by more drops than a dubstep bassline. Pressing play, she slipped the

Nano back into her top jacket pocket, brushing against the embroidered crest. Her hand then went up into her headscarf, repositioning the earbud back into her ear so she could be enveloped by music once again. She was listening to Mama's 90s playlist, and, although she would never admit it to anyone, it was certainly her favourite. *I'm a survivor . . .*

That evening, Layla couldn't stop thinking about love and forgiveness, the theme that had popped up during the day. But how could she love and forgive when people had been so awful? She decided to bring it up at dinner.

'Mama, have you ever forgiven someone who has caused you a lot of pain?'

Her mother laughed. '*Yaʒni*, I keep forgiving your father every morning for leaving the toilet seat up!' Fadia's brown eyes twinkled, and the wrinkles around her smile deepened as she teased her husband. Baba shook his head, clearly not finding it nearly as funny as Layla's mother did.

'No, Mama, seriously!'

Mama looked at Layla, her well-manicured eyebrow arching with curiosity. 'What makes you ask this question, *ah, habibti*?'

Layla shifted in her seat, her yellow cotton *jalabeeya* sticking to her legs in the hot Brisbane humidity. 'Someone said at school today that love and forgiveness are the only ways to move forward, to heal pain and all this –' Layla's voice became mocking as she made air quotes with her fingers – ' "airy-fairy" stuff.' She looked at her dad as well for reassurance. 'I don't know if forgiving someone who wants to hurt you makes any difference though.'

Baba wasn't giving her anything, and her mother's face betrayed no emotion either.

'*Aha ya shabab*,' Fadia said to everyone else at the table. 'What do you think?'

'If people talk about forgiveness, they should start also doing it themselves, shouldn't they?' Ozzie looked up from his meal for the first time that evening, his voice cutting, indicating that this meant a little something more to him. He let go of his fork and knife, ignoring them as they clattered sharply on the glass table. He looked irritated, as if Layla had said something to him personally.

Ozzie pushed his chair back from the dining table and threw his hands outward aggressively. 'Listen. If they want to talk about forgiveness, then they should take you off probation, give you your scholarship back and make Peter apologize to you for the way he treated you.' Ozzie's voice rose. 'If they want us to forgive, they should stop talking about us in the news like we are all terrorists, or gang members.' Her brother's jaw clenched, then he jumped up abruptly, and the movement tipped his chair backwards, the metal frame crashing on to the tiles, skidding across the room and loudly hitting the bannister on the wall.

Layla grimaced; that was going to leave a mark in the wood of the bannister. She looked back at her brother, who wasn't done.

'If they want forgiveness, they can start actually accepting us, hiring us, rather than wondering why we're all unemployed! That sounds like the kind of forgiveness I am interested in!' He then turned round and stormed off. His thudding footsteps could be heard climbing the staircase, walking down the hallway, and then *SLAM*; there went his bedroom door.

Layla looked round the table. Baba was unperturbed, diligently wiping up the juices of the meal with a piece of bread, all with the attitude of a man who has no problems in the world. His moustache bristled slightly, but Layla couldn't tell whether that was from annoyance, or just his chewing.

Sami and Yousif had been sitting very still, very silently, almost holding their breath. Now that Ozzie had left the table, giggles started to escape from their tightly held lips. Layla figured it was only a few minutes before they went into full-fledged laughing mode once more. They really lived in their own world.

Layla looked at her mother, who sat at the head of the table, hands clasped together on her lap. Her mother breathed in deeply, then exhaled slowly, a breath of sadness and resignation. Mama looked up at Layla. 'Don't worry about Ozzie. He's just frustrated – he's been applying for part-time jobs, but without any luck. The shopkeepers nearby said they don't want kids who could be a part of an "African gang" in their workforce. Ozzie is taking it very personally.' Her mother's voice was soft, her tone almost apologetic. 'People don't always understand what they don't know, *habibti*.'

'Yes, but that doesn't make it hurt less, does it?' Baba's voice interjected. His voice was soft, but the tone wasn't. It sounded like her dad knew exactly what Ozzie was going through. Like he knew this pain. Pursing his lips, indicating the discussion was over, Baba changed the subject. 'Everyone finished?' he asked.

Dinner is always so dramatic!

The twins nodded, then started slapping each other's shoulders in a strange game no one quite understood. Layla looked at her father and nodded as well. He started collecting the plates to put in the dishwasher.

Layla sat back in her chair. Ozzie had a point. Forgiveness had to go both ways, didn't it? But what did forgiveness even mean? And did she even have time to deal with this when she had a competition she needed to win? She looked at her mother for advice, reassurance, but her mother's mind was somewhere else. Mama was leaning forward on the table; her thick forearms resting on either side of the plate, dark brown eyes rimmed with black kohl, staring into space. Fadia's hands trembled ever so slightly, which was unusual for her. Tendrils of henna decorated Layla's mother's fingers, the artistry of vines and flowers in a dark black ink trailing across her palms and down to her wrists. The colour was faded around the tops of her fingertips, the light brown of the washed-out markings meaning Mama would probably be having her monthly henna session soon. She would spend it sitting on the couch in front of the television for hours as Safia, the local artist extraordinaire, worked her magic. Fadia's hair was freshly set in loose curls that waterfalled across her broad shoulders, which today were heaving under the pressure of holding a family up in a country she didn't always feel welcome in. Still, Fadia never hunched.

'Ma?' Layla prodded her mother with gentle words. 'Ma?' Her voice held a question.

There was no response from her mother for a beat. Then, like the air escaping a balloon, another deep sigh, and her mother collected herself, her hands no longer trembling. She picked up her plate to take to the kitchen. 'Layla, *habibti*.' The plate was loose in her hands, and she met Layla's eyes with a firm but gentle gaze. 'It's tough, *habibti*. It's tough for all of us. Focus on what you can control for now, OK?'

With that, she turned and walked away, her colourful *jalabeeya* a kaleidoscope of beauty and confusion.

Chapter 12

The rest of the week at school, all Layla could think about was the competition. The lunchtime before tech class, Layla started to get a little worried. She knew that Mr Gilvarry would ask her about the project, but she had no ideas. The competition was the best way for her to win back favour with the principal – he'd said as much on her first day back when she'd come into school – but she had no entry. She had heard that Peter's group had already moved past brainstorming and into building their first prototype, but she was nowhere near that stage! It was all a disaster, and Layla didn't know who to tell or confide in. She had tried to talk to Dina, but Dina was excited about the idea that Layla might have to leave MMGS and go back to ISB with her, so she wasn't much help. The only other person Layla felt she could trust was Ethan.

At that moment, she heard his voice – and it was as if he could read her thoughts. 'You OK, Laylz? You look kinda sad. Is everything all right?'

Layla turned her head to look at him. They were both sitting on a bench outside the tech building, nestled in the shrubbery that covered most of the building's walls. Layla had gone to pray at lunchtime and then sat down to get some air before classes were meant to start. (She may have also been trying to avoid running into Peter or his brother.)

'How did you even know I was here?' Her voice came out almost accusatory, like punches. Layla swallowed; it wasn't her intention to sound so harsh. *What's wrong with me?* Any other time, Layla would have been super excited by the chance to sit next to Ethan, alone and hidden in shrubbery. But her mind was totally occupied by the competition and the fact that her future – her whole perfectly planned-out future – was at stake.

Ethan seemed taken aback by Layla's tone. 'Oh, I saw you walk across the oval and I thought you might want some company. I knew it was you by, you know . . .' Ethan waved at the long skirt in an awkward fashion. He chuckled slightly, then fell quiet.

Oh, rah, I didn't mean to make him feel bad.

Ethan continued: 'I'm sorry, let me know if you want to be left alone. I just wanted to say that you can talk to me.' Ethan studied his fingers. A single red curl came loose and obscured his face.

The stillness held for a moment, then stretched into a minute, then two. Layla went to start to talk, but hesitated. What did she even want to tell him? That she was sad that she might lose her scholarship and get kicked out of the school? That she was angry that she was the one paying the price for something she didn't think was her fault, even if she might have had some part in it? That she needed to win this competition, but she had no idea what she was doing? That she thought he was the cutest guy she'd ever seen, but she didn't know if he liked her, or even what to do about that? So many things to say. Where should she start?

Layla opened her mouth, not sure where she was going but needing to say something, anything, to break the silence. 'Ethan, you know . . .' she began, her voice croaky.

Ethan's eyes instantly looked up from the ground, meeting hers. They were a light greeny-brown, hazel almost, with specks of gold. His pupils were large and dilated, presumably because they were sitting in shadow. His expression was expectant – nervous, almost.

'Yeh?' he asked. 'Is it about the party or something? You know, it's not a big deal if you can't make it. I'm thinking about not going either.'

The party! Layla bit back a laugh. The party was another thing that she was screwing up, but it was so low on the priority list right now. *Sigh*. She barely registered Ethan's comment about him not going.

'No, no, it's not about the party. It's, like . . .' Layla broke eye contact and turned away, her mouth still open. The words began to pour out of her mouth. 'I'm just so worried about this robotics competition, you know? I haven't even got a real idea yet, and I have to do it all by myself, and compete with the damn Cox, and I feel like I don't have a chance . . .' Layla swallowed.

Janey Mack.

The verbal diarrhoea was unstoppable. Layla ranted, as if she was at the Hussein dinner table rather than next to the boy she was crushing on, sitting on a tiny seat hidden in the shrubbery.

'It's so unfair. I don't think I did anything wrong, but I'm being punished for it, and nothing happens to him! I mean, I know I shouldn't have called him a convict . . . but C'MON! Nothing has happened to him! And nobody else seems to think it's a problem! I'm meant to pretend like this is OK or something, but I haven't even been asked for my side of the story. I came to MMGS because I thought I was welcome. I thought I was equal. I thought, at a place like this, I'd be able to learn and become a world-travelling adventurer, meeting new people, going to lots of different places, having the time of my life! Instead, I'm supposed to be proving that I deserve to be here, because the chairman's kid is a liar?

I'm supposed to bite my tongue and let that happen? I already did the exam, I proved I was worth being here – why don't they trust me? Why does everyone make these judgements about me and where I'm from just by looking at me and I don't even get a chance . . .'

Layla was almost out of breath, but she continued, ignoring her stomach tightening in knots, ignoring her brain saying, *STOP ALREADY, YOU'RE EMBARRASSING YOURSELF*, ignoring the bewildered look on Ethan's face. 'I mean, I feel like people don't want to believe me – or believe IN me! They don't want to believe people like me and my mum can look the way we do and still do everything. They don't want to believe my brother isn't in a gang. They don't want to believe I didn't pick the fight, that someone else might have. They want to make us beg to be treated well, and then they don't want us to complain, and, even then, I'm not good enough, my brother isn't good enough, *none* of us are good enough. Like, when will we be *enough*?!'

The last few words burst out of her mouth loudly, explosively. 'And everyone wants me to *forgive*?!'

With these words, she leaped up from the bench, all thoughts of her feelings about Ethan momentarily forgotten. All the frustrations of the past few weeks had come back and hit her at the same time. The unfairness of her situation, the fact that things were difficult for Ozzie, even the reality that Ms T looked white when she was black, a complicated result of the terrible things that had happened in her people's past. Layla had heard about how the government made plans to 'breed out' the blackness from Indigenous people to make them 'whiter'. The government took away lighter-skinned Indigenous children from their mothers (the group known as the 'Stolen Generations') and made the lighter-skinned people marry each other, or only white people, so there would be no black people left. It was pretty messed up.

All of it made Layla so, so, so mad. And she felt helpless. And that helplessness made her even angrier.

'I mean, do you even get it?' Layla spat at Ethan. 'Bah.' She turned round haughtily, facing the oval. 'Your parents have enough money to send you to this school. We have to send all our money to family back home. They would starve without us. You probably have no idea how hard life can be.'

The thought of her scholarship being taken away sat in the back of her mind as she surveyed the view. The enormous oval, with lush, carpet-deep green grass. Buildings that looked like they were lifted out of an architectural-magazine feature on castles. Students milling about, wearing ties and wide-brim straw hats, like they were at the polo. Layla couldn't believe she was even there. Of course she didn't belong. How had she even thought it might be possible?

Closing her eyes, she muttered under her breath in Ethan's direction, 'Life is easy for people like you.'

There it was. With those words out, Layla felt a weight being lifted off her chest. It wasn't even about Ethan, she knew. She hoped he got that too. She took a deep breath, opened her eyes and waited for his response.

Silence. Silence, except for the faint sounds of chatter and laughter from the other side of the oval. Silence, except for the sounds of a crow in the greenery behind the tech building. Silence. It felt heavy, expectant.

Oh no. What have I done? Oh no. Oh no. Oh no!

Layla's mouth clenched and she started to grind her teeth as her anxiety spread. These were thoughts she could share with Dina, who understood that life was more difficult for people like them. What was she doing talking about the hard parts of life with someone like Ethan? He wouldn't understand at all! Her face contorted as she held back the urge to cry. No, no, no! Not only would he think she was paranoid, but he would probably tell everyone else that she was, like, a racist, or something silly.

Layla closed her eyes and forced herself to face her friend, who, after this conversation, might not be her friend any more. She opened her eyes again, and her bushy eyebrows shot up.

The bench was empty. There was no one there. Ethan had left.

Layla's stomach dropped so quickly she felt nauseous. *Janey Mack!*

What had she done?

Layla needed to find Ethan, and fast. A quick glance at her watch told her there were only a few more minutes before lunch ended and everyone in her class would be headed their way. Layla didn't even want to imagine what would happen if she didn't get a chance to explain what she meant. Nothing she'd said was a lie, but she didn't mean to hurt him. *Ya Allah*, who was she becoming? It was as if she was picking fights with everyone. She wasn't even like that, though. She was just angry at how the world was treating her and the people she loved . . .

'Eth! Eth! Ethan, where are you?' Her voice was low and urgent as she walked round the shrubbery, parting the greenery every few steps to check if he had hidden inside the bushes. Then Layla started checking further afield and made her way round the back of the building. She walked along the narrow path between the building and the fence at the edge of the school boundary. The fence was nothing but wire and her hands trailed along it, following every bump. Her eyes glazed over as she stopped walking and stared into space. If only she could just run away from all these problems . . .

A movement broke her out of her reverie. Ethan was next to her, leaning against the fence.

How did this guy move so silently? Ethan!

'Ethan!' her voice and brain shouted at the same time.

'What are you doing?' he asked, nodding towards where Layla was holding on to the fence, his eyebrows quizzical.

Layla looked down and noticed that her foot was wedged into one of the holes in the mesh, and her hands were gripping the top railing as if she was about to jump over. Layla let go of the railing with surprise and stumbled backwards. 'Weird, but OK. Mate. Where were you? I was looking for you everywhere! Listen, I am so sorry about kicking off earlier, I didn't mean to get all worked up and you know it's not really about you, right . . .'

Layla trailed off as she noticed Ethan's face. He didn't look angry at her at all. 'Dude?'

He sighed, a cloud coming over his crystal-clear eyes, greener now than ever before.

'We're all hiding something, Layla. Everyone is fighting their own battle.' Ethan took in a deep breath, unexpectedly shuddering.

Holy bananas, hold up. Is he going to cry? Layla reached up to squeeze his arm, feeling the muscles tense underneath her fingers. 'Mate, what's going on?'

Before he could continue, a group of their classmates appeared round the corner. The rest of the boys were boisterous and giddy from the lunch break, and they trampled in like antelope, crushing all emotion and vulnerability in sight. The mood shifted as the air filled with the laughs and yells of young teenage boys.

'Ayyyyy, there you both are! Cheeky, hiding behind the tech building, ayyyy?' Baz galloped alongside them and ruffled Ethan's perfectly coifed curls and tugged on the end of Layla's scarf, which was flapping in the wind.

'Oi!' Ethan yelled, annoyed, knocking Baz's hand off his head. 'You don't let me touch your hair, mate. Don't touch my wonder-curls!'

Baz laughed, smirking. 'All right, all right! Anyway, it's cold out here. What's with this wind? Let's get inside!'

The herd of students thundered up the stairs, and, for a moment, Layla turned round to look back at the path, wondering what unspoken truths they had left behind.

Chapter 13

Layla was nervous. Mr Gilvarry was a great mentor, but she hadn't come up with a single idea for this project that would work, and she knew that he would ask. The teacher was late today though, as he often was when class was in the afternoon. Layla stuffed her hands in her pockets, fidgeting.

'Oi, Laylz!' Seb was sitting with her today, hissing her name from his stool on the other side of the workbench. The class was still quite noisy as Mr G hadn't arrived yet and there was an argument about who got to control the music, given Baz had already plugged his iPhone in but it was *technically* Tony's day.

'Laylz.'

She tried to ignore him.

'Laylz! Laylz!! QUEEN Laylz!'

'What?' Layla snapped. But if she was going to reply, she might as well reply to 'Queen'.

Seb leaned towards her, eyes darting from side to side furtively. 'Oi.' His voice was low, measured. Layla leaned towards Seb, almost involuntarily.

'*What?*' Her voice was lower too, but still annoyed. Seb smiled, then, from behind his back, he brought out a packet of sweets. 'Want a gummy worm?' He grinned, the gap between his two front teeth on full display. 'They're delishhhh!'

Layla leaned back on her stool, chuckling. 'You're a nincompoop, Seb. But sure, I'll have a gummy worm!' She stuffed her right hand into the offered packet, grabbed a couple and pulled them out. 'Oh, the sour ones too!' They were definitely the best. 'Thanks, Seb, I needed that.'

'I know, I could tell. Your face was sourer than those worms! Cheer up! You'll be fine, whatever it is.'

Layla's smile fell slightly, although it didn't disappear completely. Things might not always be fine, but at least she had friends who would look out for her. She had never really thought she would make friends she trusted who weren't Muslim, not until she met Adam anyway. Not because she didn't like them or anything, but, well, she'd never really known any non-Muslims. But it turned out that even if non-Muslims didn't know what it was like to be her, some would at least try to understand.

Layla's shoulders slumped. *Rah*, she was really going deep. Who was she kidding? Seb had just given her gummy worms, not a therapy session. She was being so extra right now. Plus, she'd lied to them about being allowed to go to the party on the weekend. They wouldn't understand that.

Layla clasped her hands together, elbows on the workbench, savouring the texture of the gummy worms in her mouth and ignoring the nagging voice that told her to deal with the issues she'd locked in the vault. *Nope!*

She focused on the gummy worms. The sour tang of the coating tingled her taste buds and she ran her tongue over the ridges of the worms, trying to get to every single bit of that sour-sugary stuff that made them so very delicious. Without thinking, Layla swallowed them all in one go.

Oh – God – *Ya – Allah!*

Layla tried to cough, but there was too much gummy worm stuck in her throat. She choked slightly, and her eyes bulged as she tried to force them down her throat, attempting to swallow over and over and over. Was she going to choke to death, here in the tech building, over a bundle of gummy worms?! A single tear threatened, partly out of stress and partly out of bewilderment. Layla gripped the edge of the workbench to try to calm herself down. She closed her eyes, gently, so as not to disturb the tears pooling, and silently prayed.

Ya Allah. *Please don't let me die by choking on gummy worms. I will do ANYTHING. Literally anything.*

Layla opened her eyes and tried to swallow one more time. Somehow, this time, it worked.

ALHAMDULILLAH! *Allah, THANKS FOR ANSWERING MY PRAYERS SO QUICKLY!*

The worms slid down her throat as if nothing had happened. It was either because of the praying, or the fact that they had moulded together slightly. Either way, she was grateful for the ability to breathe again.

'You all right there?' Seb piped up from next to her.

Layla turned quickly and looked at him with suspicion. Surely no one had noticed what had just happened. She had tried to stay very, very cool.

'What do you mean?' Layla asked cautiously.

'Oh well, you just looked like you were gonna die, choking on the gummy worms and all.' Seb gestured around the classroom. 'I mean, we all saw it!'

Layla looked back at the rest of the classroom and noticed what had happened during her near-death experience. Every single person in the class was facing her; some had their phones out and had clearly been recording the incident, and some were just giggling. 'Wait, you *all* saw that?' Layla asked, incredulous.

'Course we did!' Baz yelled out from across the room. 'OMG, gurl, you looked like you were gonna die! The Queen, taken down by a mere worm!'

Other voices joined in: 'I got the best bit on Snapchat, and this filter makes it look WILD!'

The entire room began bubbling with chuckles and guffaws.

Layla didn't know whether to laugh or cry. She snuck a glance over at Ethan, who was looking at her with a bemused smile. Their eyes met, and he shrugged his shoulders, as if to say: 'Well, that's that then, isn't it?'

Layla smiled back. Then, from deep within her, a giggle escaped. Relaxing, she joined the shared joy. She might as well laugh too.

The whole class was still laughing when Mr Gilvarry finally arrived. He dawdled in through the door, then stopped, surveying the scene in front of him: a roomful of students bent over, slapping their legs, clapping, heads back, laughing furiously. They weren't even laughing *at* Layla any more either. The laughter was like a contagious disease – it didn't really matter who had started it, now everyone had the giggles. It almost felt like a joke Layla was part of, not the butt of.

'Well, well, well, what do we have here?' Mr Gilvarry said, his voice booming. His beard twitched – it almost looked like he was about to join in. As he made his way towards the front of the room, the class quietened down and everyone readjusted their seats.

'Well?' Mr Gilvarry asked. 'Nobody wants to let me in on the joke? OK, then,' he continued, clearly not expecting anyone to let him in on anything, 'I'll just have to get on with it, shall I?' As he took attendance on his iPad, Layla remembered why she had been dreading this class and the smile disappeared from her face. How was she supposed to tell Mr Gilvarry she still had no idea what to work on for the competition? Maybe he would forget that she was entering, forget that she had told him she would come up with a great idea . . .

'Layla!' Gilvarry had barely taken a breath after roll call when he called out her name. 'Everyone else, continue working on your ideas for your term-one projects,' he said, as he walked to Layla's workbench.

Oh dear. It seemed like there was no chance of getting away with it at all.

'Layla, Layla, Layla.' Gilvarry stood in front of her, and although it was a conversation between the two of them, the entire class was now very interested. Out of the corner of her eye, Layla could see almost everyone eavesdropping. Everyone except for Matty – he was on Peter's team and clearly had a lot of work to do, his head buried in the sketchbook in front of him. Layla wondered what he was working on. She squinted in his direction, but her spying efforts were interrupted.

'Layla, are you listening to me?' Gilvarry asked. Layla started and refocused on Gilvarry's face. 'What have you been working on?'

Her mind froze, and so Layla blurted out the first thing that came to mind. 'GUMMY WORMS! I'm working on gummy worms, yeh . . .'

Sniggers made their way round the room. Gilvarry looked at her, his moustache twitching. 'Gummy worms? I'm not sure I understand, Layla. What do you mean?'

YA. NHAR. ABYAD. How was she going to get herself out of this one? She'd said gummy worms because they were the first thing that popped into her mind, obviously because she'd just almost died choking on them. But how on earth were they relevant to a robotics competition? And now the whole class was listening, so there was no way she could back out. She had to roll with it.

Make something up!

She tried to pretend this was one of those games they'd played in drama at her old school, where you had to improvise a character on the spot based on a random word or instruction.

'Um, well, you know . . . I wanted to make something that could be a robot, and that you can eat as well, so that it's not, like, dangerous for children and society, you know?'

Layla searched her mind quickly, thinking of all the random bits of research she'd done in the past few days. She remembered something about silicone parts, and that was kind of related to gummy worms. Maybe she would give that a go. 'You know how you can have those rubbery things, like act- act-actumacators . . .'

'An actuator? Like the part of the robot that moves?' Gilvarry clarified.

'Yes, yes, an *actuator*!' Layla quickly jumped on the word. She had no idea what it meant really, but she was sure she could make it work. 'Yeh, so I saw there were actuators made out of rubber and silicone and stuff. I thought to myself, those things look delish! But I can't eat them, you know? What if we could make actuators that you could *eat*! Then it's, like . . .' Layla paused. I mean, why would anyone want to make an edible robot? Gosh, making stuff up on the spot was *hard*. She was clearly a terrible candidate for the mafia. What did the mafia even do? She'd heard something on a TV show once –

LAYLA, you're getting sidetracked again!

Where was she? Oh yeh, gummy worms.

'. . . then it's, like, good for the environment, and you can buy these actuators for children to be part of their robots, like an accessory for a robot, you know, and when they get bored of them, rather than throwing them out, you can just . . . eat them!' With that, Layla threw her hands up with a flourish.

Eek! She held her breath, waiting for the verdict. What was Mr Miyagi-Gilvarry going to say?

Layla saw Gilvarry chuckle while he stroked his beard. She couldn't tell if he was laughing because the idea was so ridiculous and he loved it, or because the idea was *just so ridiculous*. Maybe he thought it was genius. More likely he thought it was the most hare-brained idea he had ever heard . . . but maybe *that's* what made it genius?

The room was still. The air felt hot, too hot. Layla realized she was still holding her breath, and after a few more moments, she cracked.

'Sir?!' she asked. 'What do you think? You're killing me, sir!'

Gilvarry's eyes twinkled. 'Well, Layla, it isn't quite the project I thought you were going to come up with. I'm not totally sure it fits within the piece of advice I gave you, either, to pick something that will be useful to you.'

Layla's eyes started to drop. The gamble hadn't paid off!

But Gilvarry wasn't finished yet. 'So, on first glance, it seems like an awful, doomed experiment, I'll be very honest with you, lassie.'

Yeh, clearly he hated it.

'But!' His tone changed. 'But, I guess, you've got my interest piqued! I've never heard of an edible robot before. I think the idea sounds like it has the potential to be quite . . . delicious!' He smiled, then continued. 'I think it's certainly interesting enough to warrant some more investigating. You also might need to find a way to deal with hygiene so it's properly edible,' Gilvarry mused, before he turned to the room, where everyone was obviously looking at the two of them having the conversation. 'What do the rest of you think?'

Baz yelled, 'Go get 'em, GUMMY WORM QUEEEEEEN!'

Raucousness erupted, before calming down and the class resumed as normal.

The attention now gone, Layla groaned quietly to herself as she wilted on her stool, shoulders hunching.

She had got out of the conversation unscathed, but now what was she going to do?

Seb leaned over, a lopsided smile sliding on to his face. 'You just made that up on the spot, didn't ya?' he said, the edges of his eyes creasing with mirth. He handed her the rest of the gummy worm pack. 'Here, have these. You're gonna need a lot more of these cheeky worms.'

A whimper escaped from between Layla's lips. *Janey Mack!* She'd really got herself into a pickle now.

Chapter 14

That evening at dinner, Layla was much quieter than usual. Her mind was busy, trying to figure out how she was going to get out of this situation, or make something of it. She sat at the dinner table silently, pushing the food around on her plate, eyes glazed, unaware of the conversation swirling around her. Baba was talking about some drama at the local mosque, and Mama was nodding and humming in agreement.

It was Layla's favourite meal that evening, cow-tongue stew. The Sudanese delicacy was her mother's specialty, but today Layla could barely taste a thing. The pot sat in front of her, the thick slices of cow tongue swimming in a grey-brown gravy that tasted way better than it looked. The meal was a fusion of flavours from Sudan: cardamom, coriander, garlic, pepper, some of that Maggi veggie stock that Grandma loved to use. The family only had this dish once every few months, whenever the halal butcher down the road had a fresh batch in. Cooked well, *lisaan* was tender and so scrumptious Ozzie often said it should be made illegal. It also had absolutely no bones to pick out, which made it the twins' favourite meat too! Even though it was delicious, it was apparently still 'weird'. Layla had taken a cow-tongue sandwich to ISB one day, and no one else was that impressed.

'Layla, *habibti*, are you enjoying the tongue?' Her mother's voice gently probed Layla's unusual demeanour. Fadia's hair was out of curls today and her afro was tied back in a giant puff on top of her head. She had been working long hours at the hospital, so hadn't had time to get her hair done.

Layla looked up from her plate, where she had been moving rice around with her spoon listlessly for the last fifteen minutes.

'Would you like some bread with your meal? Would that make it better? Is there something wrong with how it tastes?'

Layla flattened her lips against her teeth, then shook her head. 'Nah, the food's good, Ma. Thanks for making tongue. I'm just not super hungry today.'

'What, you trying to lose weight or something?' Ozzie interrupted, in his typically unwelcome fashion. Layla was self-conscious about her body shape sometimes, especially since her bottom was much bigger than those of the other girls at school. She hated the fact that she didn't look like the girls on Instagram, and even though Layla knew she shouldn't compare herself to others, she had found herself skipping a meal every now and again to 'watch her figure', which was obviously a silly thing to do – and a pretty silly saying, come to think of it. Unless you were standing in front of the mirror to watch yourself the whole time? *So many sayings are super weird* . . .

'Oi, nahhhh, Ozzie, don't be ridiculous.' Layla glared at her brother across the table as he leaned over for another serving of food. 'You can't just say that, you know? It's rude.'

'It's not rude if it's true!' he retorted, spooning the last large piece of tongue on to his plate and flicking gravy down the front of his white shirt. He laughed, while his mother tsk-tsked next to him.

'Ozzie, where have you got all these strange ideas, hmm?' Fadia shook her head. 'It is certainly very rude, whether it's true or not. Apologize to your sister!'

Ozzie rolled his eyes so dramatically his entire head rotated. 'Fiiiiiiiineeee,' he said, drawling out the word like it was being pulled out of him on a single string. 'I'm *sorry*,' he said, his voice heavy with sarcasm, clearly indicating he wasn't very sorry at all.

Layla rolled her eyes back. 'Whatever, Ozzie.' Boys were so lame sometimes.

Mama turned to look back at Layla. 'I haven't forgotten about you though, *ahh*?'

Mama's 'ahh' was the Sudanese version, a guttural expression that sounded of Arabic authority. Somehow Arabic authority was always more serious than English authority.

'What's going on?' Layla's dad, who had been busily focused on the last vestiges of cow tongue on his plate, made a low grunt, adding his voice to her mother's. Without even looking up from the plate, he added, *'Aha yalla*, what's got your tongue?' He chuckled to himself at the pun. 'Did something happen at school with Peter again?'

Layla sighed, putting her spoon down next to her plate and then placing both hands beneath her legs, to stop herself from gesticulating too wildly. Her hands felt warm and safe, squeezed in between her thighs and the embroidered chair cushion.

'Well, I told Mr Gilvarry about a project idea . . .'

At this, Sami and Yousif perked up and looked at each other. They had been poking at each other's plates, pushing the tongue pieces around so the other couldn't get to them, but the mention of the project had them excited.

'Oh cool!' they said simultaneously, then started to bop up and down on their seats, clapping. 'Yayayayaya! Layla has a cool invention idea!'

'No, stop!' Layla said, her hands involuntarily leaving their warm spot between the cushion and her thighs, flying up and bunching themselves into fists on either side of the chair. 'No, that's the problem! I don't have an idea, and so I made something up on the spot, and it's something that doesn't even make sense! And now –' Layla's voice broke. She hadn't realized how upset she was until she'd started talking about it – 'and now . . . now, everyone knows about it! And everyone is going to expect me to come up with something awesome and exciting and something that works and I have no idea what I am DOING!'

With that, Layla's hands flew on to her face as she tried to stop the tears from falling. *Ya Allah*, this wasn't how it was supposed to go! She was supposed to come up with a brilliant idea, win the competition, prove them all wrong and hold on to her scholarship. Now she was stuck with an idea she knew was doomed to fail, and she didn't even know how to get started!

Silence fell around the table, punctuated only by Layla's sniffles.

'Layla, Layla . . .' the twins piped up, their voices high. 'What is the idea?'

'*Aywa*,' said Baba. 'Let's hear the idea before we get too caught up in whether or not it's a good one, mmm?'

Layla wiped the tears from her eyes and looked down at her hands. The indents that her jeans had made on the tops of her fingers were visible, and a few small hairs popped out just underneath her knuckle sitting crooked. 'Well . . .' She took a deep, shuddering breath. 'Well, I told Mr Gilvarry that I could make a robot actuator out of edible gummy worms.'

Silence fell around the table again, but this time there seemed to be slight confusion.

Then Sami jumped up. 'Did you say gummy worms?'

Yousif followed. 'Like those delicious things we get from the shop down the road?'

Layla nodded.

'You're going to make robots out of gummy worms?' they both said together excitedly, eyes wide. 'YAYYYYYYY!!!'

Bless their little bamboo socks. They were always so enthusiastic about everything she did. Of course they thought it was a good idea. Delicious edible robots would definitely be exciting for a couple of kids. But an edible actuator was not useful to anyone else. Layla turned to look at her mother and father, secretly hoping they would contradict the story she was telling herself, secretly hoping they would be just as excited as the twins, but they were not.

Her mother and father were both looking at her with befuddled expressions.

I don't think I've ever seen this combination of faces before! Layla's mind registered the moment as funny, despite the misery of the situation.

Even Ozzie had paused, his hand halfway to his mouth, the bread and cow tongue in his fingers forgotten as he squinted at his little sister, trying to figure out if it was a joke. The gravy from the tongue dripped down on to his white shirt, but nobody noticed.

'What . . . ? What . . . ?' Her dad shook his head, as if it would help him understand the situation better. 'How did you go from making something useful, like a tool to help weed the patio, to something so random, like an actuator that you might be able to eat? How would you even be able to make it safe to eat?' Baba leaned back in his chair. 'Although, that being said, I am glad you know what an actuator actually is. That's a win!'

Chapter 15

Layla had a plan. She dropped her enormous backpack (full of Mr Gilvarry's books that she hadn't read!) at the 8A homeroom, then grabbed a book about material design that Gilvarry had given her and made her way towards the tech building. Even though the idea was a little bit ridiculous even to her, she was determined to make something of it. Maybe she would discover something exciting and exotic, kind of like how penicillin was discovered. That was what she told Mama anyway, every time she wanted to avoid doing the dishes. 'I'm just following in the footsteps of the great doctor, I mean Sir Alexander Fleming, Ma, who made his biggest discovery because of some dirty dishes!' Her mother remained unconvinced that Layla neglecting her chores was going to make her the next Alexander Fleming. Well, it was her mother's loss, Layla had concluded.

Textbook tucked under her arm, she strode across the oval towards the tech building. Her long maroon skirt made a flapping sound as she walked. Layla hated that sound in this new school – it announced her presence and made her feel conspicuous whenever she was walking in a group with anyone else. Like a squeak in a shoe, it was slightly embarrassing for some reason. All the other girls had shorter skirts, and those never made any noise at all.

But Layla had learned to adjust, as she always did. And clearly the skirt wasn't impeding her speed in any way, because she cut across the oval in record time, hurried by the thought of what possible robot inventions she could work on. Yes, she was worried about the scholarship; yes, she missed Dina; yes, she really wanted to go to that party but didn't think she was going to be able to and needed to come up with a decent excuse fast; yes, she hated what Peter had put her through; and yes, she had no idea of what she was doing with this gosh darn gummy worm project – or GORM for short – but if there was one thing Layla did love, it was an adventure, and a problem to solve. And by golly wasn't this a problem to solve. *Channel the* JAMEL*!*

Layla reached the building and collected a bunch of skirt material in one hand, lifting the hem almost up to her knee, before she bounded up the stairs to the tech room. She was quite the sight, hijab flying as she sidestepped left to right up the steps, deftly avoiding drips of water from the rock above, a look of joy on her face. Layla loved moments like these – quiet seconds where she imagined she was part of a movie sequence or a video game. The drips of water were toxic waste and the walls were closing in, threatening to crush her if she didn't get up to the next level in time. Here, in her imagination, the floor was lava, and she was the only one with the unique set of skills and gifts to pass this level and proceed to the next stage of the game. She had speed, agility and protective armour (her hijab). She was Layla, the Queen.

The tech room was dim as she approached, and the lights flickered on as she walked through the door, switched on by her movement. With the light came the familiar hum of fluorescent lights warming up, and Layla looked around, eyes adjusting to the space. She breathed in deeply, taking in the smell of pine and varnish, silicone and steel. The possibilities in this room were endless – it was like walking into a pantry with all the raw materials and utensils to bake any kind of dessert you wanted. Where did you start, when you had all the options to make anything?

But she wasn't here to think about woodwork – that would be for another time. Layla walked to the middle of the room and pulled up a stool at the central table, popped herself on it and cracked open the book in front of her. Dust flew out, specks visible in the ray of light coming through the windows in the roof. The book smelled musty, and as Layla flicked through, some pages were stuck together from age.

Hmm, there must be something in here about edible materials. She tried the index and checked 'e' for 'edible'. It was so weird not being able to press Control + F and find what she needed, but she had to do this the old-school way.

But what was she even looking for? Layla put the textbook down on the workbench, the thick hardback making a loud slapping noise against the benchtop and sending more dust flying. She coughed, waving her hands in front of her in an effort to disperse the dust cloud. Pursing her lips, she leaned back on the stool, her hands gripping the stool legs for balance, and then pushed back, so only two of the stool feet were touching the concrete workshop floor. Layla searched her memory for something that might be useful. What was that material she was researching that was kind of like a gummy worm?

Ah! Silicone!

Releasing her hands, she threw her weight forward to keep the stool from tipping, almost losing balance completely. *Wah!* Layla threw her hands forward, her fingertips gripping the edge of the workbench to stop herself from falling over completely. She laughed to herself quietly, looking around to make sure nobody had seen her nearly completely stack it. Fortunately, the room was still very empty and silent, except for the faint sound of a kookaburra – a loud Australian bird – laughing outside.

Layla licked her index finger – oh, the taste of dust! – and started flicking through the index again, looking for silicone. Page 315, the index informed her. Good Lord, there was a whole chapter on silicone. This was perfect.

Layla spent the next hour reading about silicone: how it worked, what it was used for, how it was made. She heard a few faint sounds in the distance, but paid little attention to them, too lost in understanding the silicone moulding process.

I guess I can just think of gummy worms as silicone, yeh? If she was able to melt some gummy worms together, surely it would be the same as silicone. It was that rubber stuff at the bottom of the shower door that kept the water from leaking out. What was she going to make though?

Layla thought back to the first tech lesson and remembered what Mr Gilvarry had said about brainstorming. Nobody's first idea was spectacular so it was important to keep redesigning and reiterating.

He'd told them to fill their sketchbooks with their thought processes, failed ideas and brilliant solutions.

Layla fetched her sketchbook, then looked around for a pen or pencil to start sketching. Aha! There was a pencil lying on one of the other workbenches, seemingly forgotten by someone. Layla picked it up and rolled it between her fingers, savouring its round, smooth surface. Something about beautifully shaped objects made her happy, and this pencil, with its matt-black finish and elegantly simple design, drew her in. She cracked open the sketchbook, flicked over to an empty page, then ran her hands over the crisp white sheets. Taking a deep breath, she wrote neatly at the top of the right-hand page: 'Brainstorming: Gummy Worm Actuator'. The pencil made a satisfying sound as she titled the page, and she smiled and began to sketch.

Her pencil ran across the paper, taking on a life of its own. Time passed, then there was a rattling behind her and suddenly the workshop door slammed open.

'Layla! There you are. We've been looking all over for you! We almost called your parents.'

Mr Gilvarry and Ms T were standing in the doorway, the sunlight casting shadows into the room, making them stark silhouettes. Layla sat back from the sketchbook and faced the pair, startled. 'What's going on?' she asked.

'Well, you missed first period – do you know what time it is?'

Layla looked at the clock on the wall. Whoa! It was almost morning tea – where had the time gone?

'Oh no!' Layla dropped the pencil and clasped her hands over her mouth. 'I've been sitting here all morning?' she asked incredulously. 'I'm so sorry, I must have lost track of time!'

'It's fine now that we've found you, but you will have to catch up on your missed maths lesson,' Ms T said kindly.

She really wasn't so bad. The two of them had bonded since their chat about forgiveness.

'Mr Gilvarry has told me you're working hard on a robot for the Grand Designs Tourismo – is that what you've been doing?'

Layla nodded. 'It's not going very well so far, but I was doing some brainstorming sketches,' she said, gesturing at the book in front of her.

'Sketches are a great idea. Good to know you were listening in class, Layla,' Gilvarry said, his large frame now inside the room, propped up against a workbench. 'How are you going?' He strained his eyes to look at the sketchbook, and then chuckled. 'It looks like you still need a bit of help there, lass!'

Layla sighed before pressing her lips together. One side of her mouth involuntarily pulled up into a half smile as she shrugged.

'Yeh, I'm still working on the idea. I mean, I know I want to make it out of gummy worms, but I want it to be more than just an actuator. I want to make the actuator, like, do something.'

Ms T furrowed her brows. 'What *is* an actuator, Layla?'

Layla smiled. She had done a bit of research last night, just for moments like this.

'Well, Ms T,' she started, straightening her back and assuming a formal voice, 'an actuator is, like, a kind of motor that's responsible for moving something. It converts types of energy into motion.' She paused, and her eyes looked to Mr Gilvarry for confirmation.

He nodded, and Layla continued explaining, relieved, 'The energy can come from something like air, electricity, water, heat or magnets. The actuator takes that energy and makes something move.'

Ms T nodded slowly. 'Oh, OK,' she said. 'So, what would be the point of making a gummy worm actuator?'

This was the question Layla wasn't sure she had an answer to, but she gave it a go.

'Well, they'll be edible – and who doesn't want to eat part of a robot!' Layla forced a grin on her face.

She was going to make this work, whether it had a point or not! Ms T smiled and nodded, though she didn't seem that convinced.

Hmm, I might have to work on my marketing skills.

Though it seemed Mr Gilvarry wasn't so interested in the purpose of the actuator as much as he was in the technical side of things.

'Have you thought about what energy source you will use to activate it?' he asked.

Layla shook her head.

'OK. Well, in this workshop, you have access to both air and electricity, so I'd start by thinking about those options.' Gilvarry motioned to the pneumatic air hose coiled at the back of the workshop near the hand tools.

Layla had thought it was a firehose, but closer inspection indicated otherwise.

'Pneumatic will probably be easier and safer and, well, possibly more inventive,' Gilvarry mused.

Layla squinted her eyes, trying to imagine what would happen.

'So, like, I should design something that we can pump air into so that it can make the whole thing move in a certain way?' she asked. Her teacher nodded.

She couldn't believe that she had the beginnings of an idea that could work!

Gilvarry, who had wandered off towards the pneumatic hose and rig set-up, turned back and projected his voice across the room. 'I think you're on to something!' he boomed, echoes bouncing off the walls.

Ms T, who had settled on to a stool on the work-bench next to Layla, stood up. 'All right, Layla. It's time to get back. I won't report you this time because I know you were here working hard, but you can't make a habit of skipping class, OK?'

Layla internally breathed a sigh of relief. She really was shocked that so much time had passed without her realizing it, but she couldn't afford to get into more trouble right now.

'Do I have to go back to class?'

Ms T looked at Gilvarry, who shrugged.

'Well, class is almost over so you can probably go get your morning tea. But I will definitely see you after the bell rings, yes?' Ms T was kinder now for sure, but Layla heard the gentle command in her statement: make sure you come to class, or there will be trouble!

Layla nodded and collected the sketchbook to return to the cupboard.

'Oh no, no. Take that with you!' Gilvarry said. 'You don't know when inspiration will strike!'

With that, Layla bounded out of the classroom, materials book and sketchbook under her arm, 2B pencil in her fist. Her feet took her to the lunch spot on the hill, where she'd first met the boys.

Someone was already sitting on the hill! She froze, hoping that it wasn't Peter, but the boy's red curls identified the figure as Ethan.

Chapter 16

Ethan?

What was he doing sitting all by himself before the break had even started? He had his head resting on his knees, face forlorn. As Layla rushed up the hill, her noisy skirt announced her arrival and Ethan woke from his reverie.

'Whatchya doing?' Layla asked chirpily, hiding her jitters. She crouched down next to Ethan and also drew her legs up to her chest, sitting in a similar position to him. Being so close to her crush still made her nervous, but she was doing her best to mask it. Also, they hadn't really sorted things out from yesterday. Layla knew he'd read her messages last night, but he hadn't replied, so she'd been anxious about this moment. Was he still mad at her outburst?

Ethan turned his head to look at Layla, his ear now on his knee. 'Hey, Queen Laylz,' he said, his voice low and grey. 'Where were you this morning?'

'Ha!' Layla laughed, also breathing an internal sigh of relief. At least he wasn't going to ignore her. She could work with that. 'Yeh, nah, man. Ms T and I are good now, didn't I tell ya?'

Layla wondered why Ethan looked like he had just seen a ghost.

'Why are you out here all by yourself?'

Ethan turned his head away from Layla, breaking eye contact. He stared down between his knees at the ground, eyes wide open, not blinking, not making a single sound. Seconds ticked away. The sound of crickets grew louder.

'Ethan?' Layla asked, now worried. He was acting super weird, and she got the feeling it might be about something else, something more than just their chat yesterday. He *had* been acting a bit strange yesterday before everyone turned up actually. Layla realized she was holding her breath. She blinked. Ethan didn't. She started humming to break the silence, maybe annoy him into a response. Still nothing.

'Ethan!'

Layla watched, shocked, as tears began to well up in her friend's eyes. It was clear he was trying to hold them back but was failing horribly. The pools grew and wobbled, so gently and precariously, at the edges of his pink eyelids. Then, the dam broke. Rivers of tears began streaming down Ethan's face. Streams of emotion navigated freckles and pimples as they made their way down and dripped off his chin. Ethan buried his head in his arms, stifling the noise of his sobs.

'Ethan, oh my God, are you OK? Oh, *habibi* . . .' Tentatively, Layla lifted her right hand from the grass in between them and placed it ever so gently on Ethan's back. She felt his body react, then relax, and so took that as permission to pat him comfortingly, and slowly started to rub his back in circles. 'Shhhhhh,' she crooned softly to him, in the same way she would try to calm her girlfriends when they cried.

Layla moved a little closer to Ethan, so their bodies were almost touching and placed her left hand on his leg.

Rahhhhh, I don't even know if this is halal. Ah well, he's my friend, and he's sad. Allah can forgive that!

'It's going to be OK, it's going to be OK, Ethan. Whatever it is. Let it all out, it's OK.'

Layla continued to rub his back and whisper kind words to her friend until she heard the sniffling slow down and eventually stop. After a few minutes, he lifted his head and Layla pulled both of her hands back to her lap, almost guiltily. She was certainly feeling self-conscious about how close she was to Ethan now. But she tried to keep her mind on the issue at hand. This all couldn't be about her outburst yesterday. Something else was going on.

Ethan wiped the tears off his face, using his shirt collar to dry his cheeks.

'I'm sorry about that,' he said, avoiding eye contact with Layla.

'Sorry?' Layla sounded taken aback. 'Sorry for what?'

Ethan's voice, still husky from crying, was embarrassed. 'Sorry for making a scene. Sorry for crying. Sorry for being so weak, I suppose. Boys aren't supposed to cry and all that.' As he talked, he faced away from Layla, so she had to lean towards him to hear what he was saying.

'Don't be ridiculous,' Layla admonished, almost annoyed.

Urgh, she hated rules about what girls and boys were 'supposed' to do. Usually she got annoyed when someone told her girls shouldn't do something, but this was kind of the same thing.

'Dude. What is it, 1950? My dad cries ALL. THE. TIME. He cries in movies. He cried in *High School Musical*. He cried in *Moana*. He cried in *Happy Feet Two*. He cries when I win awards. He cries watching Jake Paul on YouTube, but I think that's a different kind of crying, to be honest. I don't think crying is a boy or girl thing. It's a feelings thing – and boys have feelings, don't they?' She hadn't meant it to turn out like a lecture, but clearly it was starting to sound like one, as Ethan had turned to look at her, leaning back.

His facial expression was both confused and quizzical. 'Whoa, I clearly got you going there, Laylz. I didn't mean anything by it you know, it's no big deal. You're always so dramatic . . .'

Layla shook her head. 'No, it *is* a big deal, Eth! You gotta be OK with, like, having feelings! I did an assignment about this for school last year –' in fact, this project had won her a national award, but she wasn't one for boasting – 'and it was about mental health and, like, suicide, and how, like, boys end up doing terrible things and hurting themselves because they're depressed, and, well . . . don't talk about their feelings! I don't want you to hurt yourself, Eth!'

Oh, that really had escalated. As the words were coming out of her mouth, she had seen Ethan's red eyebrows rising, higher, higher, higher . . . almost disappearing back into his hairline. When she finished, his face was stuck in an expression of shock.

'BRUH.' Ethan's eyes were wide open, and his shock exasperated Layla.

'What?! It's, like, something we gotta talk about!'

'No, I mean —' Ethan lifted his hand from the grass and gestured. 'Look behind you.'

Layla turned round and her jaw dropped. Peter had been standing behind her. Peter's presence was like a dark cloud passing through on a sunny day; his frame blocked out the sunlight and the temperature felt a little cooler in his shadow. His sleeves were rolled up — uniform regulation breach — and he had a bemused look of smugness on his face. The expression made his face ugly.

'Talking about *feelings* are you, you little worm?' he sneered. 'Well, you can talk all about those feelings when you feel what it's like to be beaten by *me* in the Grand Designs Tourismo.'

Layla rolled her eyes. She didn't have time for Peter right now, and, strangely enough, the conversation with Ethan about feelings had planted a seed in her mind about why Peter might hate her so much. Also, he had said 'worm'. Did he *know* something?

'Whatevs. Are you going to sit down and eat, or just stand around trying to look like a big man?' Her voice came out flippant, dismissive. Layla then looked back to Ethan again, turning her back on Peter and effectively ending the conversation. A tense beat passed and Layla waited, knowing this was a defining moment. Would he yell at her, push her, try to continue the battle? Or would he decide to sit down and be part of the group?

'OIIIIII!!' A yell came from far away, breaking the tension. It was Seb, running from the direction of the classroom. They all turned to watch Seb trot up the hill, his trademark brown hair flopping about, flanked by the rest of their crew.

'You guys left me alone in class!' he said, part jokingly, part accusingly. When he arrived at the top of the hill, puffed and with a bead of sweat forming on his upper lip, he stopped and then surveyed the group.

'What's going on here?'

He looked between Layla and Peter. Layla was sitting on the grass with her back to Peter, who was standing with his hands on his hips. Seb shook his head and laughed.

'Oh, whatever, hey, I just wanna *eat*! Sit down already!' Seb pushed past Peter, rocking him slightly, and then threw himself on to the grass next to Ethan. Layla laughed; Seb lay on the grass like it was his lounge room. Peter turned round and then skulked away.

Yeah, go on, get out of here! Layla turned her attention back to her friends. Seb was doing his food announcement.

'All right, everyone, we've got my *favourite* food — *arroz con pollo*!'

The boys groaned, although that was no surprise — they groaned every mealtime. Seb twisted the Crockpot lid off and then tilted the container so Layla could see inside. There was rice and chicken, and the smell of spice was *strong* but delicious.

Later, when the bell for class rang, Layla looked over at Ethan, who she'd temporarily forgotten in all the hullabaloo. His face was paler than usual, making his freckles pop like flecks of blood in snow. Even his lips looked white. His eyes stared intensely at nothing — his stillness was frightening Layla. She hadn't seen anything like this before and didn't know what was the right thing to do.

'Ethan.' She shook his shoulder. 'Ethan, it's time to go to class now.'

Ethan looked up at Layla, unseeing, got up from the grass and started walking down the hill and following the boys who had already headed off. Seb hung back and looked sideways at Layla.

'Yo,' he said, motioning to Ethan with his head. 'Figure out what's going on?'

Layla shrugged. 'I dunno, man. Was he like this in the morning?'

Seb chuckled. 'Yeh, I noticed you missed first period,' he said, then his chuckle vanished. 'He came in this morning like that, man, like he'd seen Casper or something. He didn't talk all morning, and you weren't there to, like, make a terrible joke or something to get him to laugh – even if it was out of pity. I was stuck!'

Layla started walking down the hill, laughing as her walk turned into a skip. 'Ha! Mate, you couldn't survive without me. Admit it, I'm the best thing that happened to all of youse!'

Seb jogged down beside her, shaking his head. 'Mate, nobody says "youse". It's, like, not a real word.'

Layla glared at Seb jokingly, then stopped skipping and turned round.

'Dude!' she yelled, pointing back up the hill. 'You forgot your Crockpot!'

'Oh, for the love of God!' Seb yelled, and started jogging back up the enormous hill. Layla's cackle followed Seb all the way back up. 'When you hear that sound, really, it can only be Layla.'

The bell rang for the end of the final class just as Layla was thinking about her gummy worm design again. Everyone rushed to their bags, and while stuffing her books into her backpack, Layla realized that Ethan hadn't left his seat and was staring into space. He hadn't said anything all afternoon either. She walked towards him.

'Broooo, what's going on?' she asked. 'C'mon, man. It's home time! Let's go!' She waved for him to join her.

Ethan slowly got out of his chair, tucked it under the desk meticulously and started walking to the door. Layla, ever impatient, walked behind him, then even more impatiently started pushing him in the back to walk faster.

Ethan spun round suddenly. 'Get off me!' he said, flicking her hands away.

He turned and continued walking, but Layla stood still, shocked. Ethan didn't seem like the sort of person who *ever* lost his temper or cool – not even in a joking way. He'd always been quite quiet and level-headed since Layla had known him.

'Ethan, Ethan, wait!' Layla ran after him, her backpack thudding heavily with every step. The long skirt and backpack combination wasn't doing her any favours in the aerodynamics department. Standing in front of Ethan, Layla looked down, studying her scuffed brown leather shoes.

'Listen, I'm sorry,' she whispered. 'I shouldn't have touched you without asking, and I definitely shouldn't have pushed you. I don't know what's going on –' Layla looked up from her fingers into his face, meeting his eyes briefly before looking back down – 'but know that I'm here for you when you're ready to tell me, OK?'

Ethan sucked his lips in and nodded silently. Layla stood awkwardly in front of him, unsure.

'Well, then . . . I can't do much, but can I give you a hug?' she asked him.

Again, Ethan nodded wordlessly.

Layla reached round and enveloped Ethan in a hug – of friendship, of comfort, of . . . well, she was hugging the guy she had a crush on, so it was a hug of *so* much!

Letting go, she smiled at him. 'OK, I gotta run. Text me, OK?'

Ethan nodded.

Layla trotted out of the classroom and towards the front gate.

Something about that hug had planted another seed in her mind. So at home that night, lying in bed, her mind wandering, Layla held her breath for a moment then sat up with excitement. She had an idea.

That was it!

Chapter 17

'I'm going to make an edible robot that gives you hugs!' Layla announced with a flourish the next morning before class. She was in the tech room, sketchbook open, talking to Mr Gilvarry, who had come in to check on her progress.

'It's perfect, because the only things that have to move are the arms, so I can make a bear or a doll out of anything.' Layla's arms were animated as she excitedly tried to outline in the air what the thing she invented would look like. Her beige blouse was covered with bits of blue rubber that had come off the eraser as she drew and redrew ideas. The side of her hand was also darkened with lead where it had been rubbing on the sketches she had drawn in the book.

Mr Gilvarry watched Layla with amusement, and his ginger moustache bristled with pride. Finally, she had connected with an idea that made sense to her.

'Maybe something else edible, like a gingerbread cookie or something?' suggested Gilvarry.

'Yeh! Like that!' Layla exclaimed, clapping excitedly and sending the pencil in her hand flying, clattering across the room. 'And then you attach the arms to the doll or bear, and you make the arms so, once they're actuated they go from being straight to arms that come up and give you a hug!' Layla looked down at her notes thoughtfully. 'Or maybe the robot could just give a soft-drink can a hug because right now making a big robot is probably a little too much?'

Her mouth twisted in amusement. This was going to be *so dope*! No one else was going to have a robot like hers. And she had come up with it all by herself too – being a solo team was the actual best!

She'd had the idea when she was hugging Ethan. She remembered feeling all stiff and heavy – her backpack felt like it was weighing her down with stones so her upper body couldn't really move; her long skirt was stiff and heavy, and her blazer was almost as bad. Even then, she didn't need all that much to be able to give a hug! She just needed to move her arms. And with that small movement, something magical happened – her friend felt better! So that night, as she lay in bed, her brain had joined the dots. Why not create something simple, to copy something that she had experienced joy from in real life? And also to show people the importance of hugs, of taking care of each other and of friends. It could be a gift. You could even put a little note in the gummy bear's arms, that would be a nice touch, and, like, wayyyy cooler than one of those weird gift cards that sing. And once you've shown people, well, then you can eat it!

She *really* loved eating gummy worms. Ha! Ms T thought a gummy actuator would be useless. Wait till she heard about this! Layla had wriggled excitedly underneath her quilt, then decided she couldn't wait until the morning. Leaping out of bed, she fumbled and searched in the darkness for her schoolbag, fishing out her sketchbook and a pencil. Creeping silently back into her bed, the floor creaking slightly, she used the torch on her phone to light up an empty page and scribble at the top:

INTRODUCING: HUGGY BEAR!

It would be weird to call it a huggy worm, and I really want to make it a play on words of some sort! This will do.

Singing to herself, she had scribbled a few sketches on her page hurriedly that night. Starting with a very basic block with moveable arms, she'd changed it to the shape of a person, to a Lego woman with silicone / gummy-worm arms. The drawings were sloppy and rough, but Gilvarry would be pleased, she knew. It didn't need to look pretty, it just needed to explain what she was trying to show. And if a stick figure worked, a stick figure worked!

Back at the workshop, Layla was negotiating the next steps with Gilvarry. She had pages and pages of sketches now and had a fairly good idea of what she wanted it to look like.

'Nice one, young 'un,' Gilvarry said, smiling as Layla showed him the sketches. 'Just in time too! You'll have to work hard to get the thing built by competition day next week, but if you put your head down, you should just make it! Phew!' Gilvarry rubbed his hands together, clearly pleased for his student.

Layla was sure she'd misheard the man. 'Next *week*?! What do you mean the competition is next week?' As she saw Gilvarry nod, Layla could barely contain her shock. She hadn't had a clue the deadline was so close.

'How is it so soon?'

This might be the perfect excuse to get out of the party though . . .

'Well, you see, most of the project teams start working before the Christmas break, because they know the competition date is so early in the school year. And usually new people join an existing team, so it doesn't make that much of a difference. For you, however, you're in a unique position. Didn't you check when you signed up?'

Layla absentmindedly shook her head, not really listening.

Gosh, she really had been stuffing up a lot of things since she'd started at MMGS. Forgetting to go to class, suspension, now almost missing the competition date. She knew this place would have lots of new opportunities, but she had never really thought about all the extra work and responsibilities that came with that.

Gilvarry also mentioned something about signing up. I should probably find out what he was talking about . . .

But before Layla could even finish that thought, her mind slipped into Shutdown Mode. It was the phrase 'the competition is next week' that triggered her brain into that infamous method of focus she had used at ISB, and the very same one that had helped her study hard enough to get the MMGS scholarship. This wasn't a normal race any more, this was a hardcore sprint to the finish line. She needed to work hard and fast to ensure she smashed this thing out of the park. Since Shutdown Mode was now activated, there would be no time for idle chatter. Mr Gilvarry seemed to be going on and on about paperwork. Layla looked at him and watched his mouth move, but she had totally tuned out his words.

'Just remember to submit your forms,' he was saying. 'And the way it works is that there is a first round, where the judges look at the different robots. Only twenty-five per cent go to the next round, and then it's a bunch of elimination rounds until they pick the winner. You can join forces with people after the first round if you don't make it through –'

'All right, Mr G. I'm off!' she announced, cutting him off mid-sentence. She was never going to join someone else's team.

Gilvarry looked slightly shocked, like he was surprised Layla was leaving at that exact moment, but she didn't have time to stick around. She needed some alone time – to sit down, make the prototype, and win this competition, proving to everyone that she deserved to be there.

Layla ran out of the room, feet sliding on the smooth concrete floor, skidding slightly, and she bolted down the hall. She just liked breaking out into a sprint sometimes: it gave her a burst of energy and kept things interesting. She sang to herself as she ran, adding a score to her own superhero saga.

As she hopped down the stairs, no hands on the handrails – because she was risky like that – the bell for first period rang in the distance. *Aiiieee!* She was going to have to run to class and finish the drawing of the prototype later. There would be no time for chatting during morning tea or lunch either now, given she was in Shutdown Mode. It was all hands on deck.

While she ran, she DM'd Dina.

Multitasking!

Layla:	*Gurl, things are getting hectic.*
	I'm going into SD mode.
Dina:	*SHUTDOWN MODE? Yo,*
	things must be real bad.
Layla:	*Yeh. Imma be offline for a bit.*
Dina:	*I can't c u this w/e? not comin*
	2mosque on Sun?
Layla:	*Nah, boo soz :/*

Dina:	*Guess that's ur excuse for that party too . . .*
Layla:	*Ha. Silver linings?*

That afternoon, sitting back on a stool in the tech room, feet resting on the bar between the stool legs, Layla surveyed the page in front of her and grinned, pleased.

Perfect.

The drawing was the seventh Huggy Bear she had sketched that afternoon. She'd started with a plain gingerbread man as suggested by Mr Gilvarry, but she didn't think that was enough. How could she make it more real? This was supposed to be, like, a robot competition, not *MasterChef*!

After the fourth sketch, which had looked suspiciously similar to the first sketch, Layla had flicked the pencil out of her fingers with frustration. Unsure of where to progress, she had fingered the beads on her necklace hidden underneath her blouse.

Man, I miss making jewellery. Jewellery was easy, you simply came up with a pattern and then threaded beads on to some string. If you really wanted to go wild, you could make a pattern with the string, almost like knitting, before threading the beads on – but still, it was basically beads on string. Some of her earring ideas were a little more exotic and inventive, and Layla enjoyed playing around with different sizes of beads, various colours and unusual materials. She had once made earrings out of small bolts and nuts, and they looked *really* cool, except they were so heavy that they made her ears bleed. That got Layla thinking. Maybe there was some way of building this bear in the same way she made jewellery?

Layla focused her eyes on the sheet in front of her, wiped the surface of the page for good luck, said a quick prayer (*Bismillah*) and started sketching.

Layla had realized that jewellery was all about patterns and modules – she just took many pieces that looked the same and put them together in a way that made something new. Why couldn't she do the same with this?

So the seventh version of the Huggy Bear that stared up at her from the page was exactly that: a bear made out of edible parts that you could put together easily to make something greater.

I've just made a robot out of edible Lego. Haha!

The 'parts' or 'ingredients' were simple: the basic building block was a liquorice cube, held together by wooden skewers that Layla knew she had at home for barbeques. The skewers were like the string in jewellery, and the liquorice acted like the beads. Layla *loved* liquorice, so it wasn't hard to think of that as the basic building 'bead'. The liquorice made up the body and legs of the bear, the arms were made out of gummy worms melted together (that would be the actuator), and the head, well, the head gave Layla a bit of trouble. She wanted the head to be half of a chocolate egg or something, but she couldn't think how to attach it to the neck and body. She couldn't poke a skewer through a chocolate egg, because the chocolate would explode into tiny, useless pieces. As she was thinking, Layla started chewing the end of the pencil, a habit she'd picked up when studying for her scholarship test. *Shame I don't have a lollipop I could chew instead* . . . She surveyed the damage she'd done to the pencil after a few minutes. *Lollipop!*

That was it. The bear's head was going to be made out of a lollipop. The neck and head joint would be taken care of, and the lollipop stick could pierce straight into the liquorice cube. It was perfect!

Layla surveyed the sketch in front of her and pursed her lips. She wasn't sure this was going to work, but she liked the fact that every single part of this weird delicious contraption was edible, so even if she didn't win, at least she'd get a treat at the end of it.

The shape of the Huggy Bear sorted, it was now time to focus on the actual robot part – the edible actuator arms. Layla knew from her research that she'd need to use some sort of mould to cast the shape she envisioned. She also had a pretty good idea of what she wanted the arms to do – to go from being straight while resting at the sides of the bear, to arms that lifted up, almost to shoulder level, and then curled in, as if it was giving a hug.

Furrowing her brow, Layla turned to a new page and wrote: 'THE ACTUATOR ARMS' in big bold letters at the top. *Pretty cool!* Then, she sketched. She sketched all kinds of possible arm shapes and sizes, scribbled notes in the margins, some relevant and some completely unrelated.

'Arms need to be able to curve' was scribbled next to 'Be brave!', which she was trying to remind herself of, and 'Allah has your back!' then 'Channel the *jamel*!', her mantra. Layla drew everything and anything that came to mind, because that's what Mr Gilvarry said good brainstorming was.

With that philosophy, Layla filled pages and pages with sketches, and slowly got close to what she thought it would be possible to make. The final draft sketch looked familiar. Layla closed her eyes and tried to imagine what it was that the drawing reminded her of. Ah! It looked like when she took a tray of ice cubes out of the freezer, but it had over-filled and so all the ice cubes were joined together. But in Layla's sketch, it was a single row of ice cubes – or, in reality, melted together gummy worms – that were all connected, making it strong but also flexible.

Layla needed to try to make it to see if it worked! First, she had to find a small novelty ice-cube tray to try as a mould, and then she would have to melt the gummy worms together and test it all out.

Satisfied with that plan of action, Layla glanced down at her right wrist and checked the time on her watch. *Crikey!* Time had flown by, and if that time was right, Baba had been waiting out front for something like half an hour! She packed her sketchbook and pencils into the bag in a hurry. *Oh dear, I'm going to get in so much trouble.*

This was turning out to be a theme for Layla.

As she ran across the oval to the front of the school, her mind felt at ease for the first time since she had been suspended. Shutdown Mode had helped. Now everything was under control: she had a plan for the project, she knew what she needed to do, she could see the path to success. Even though she hadn't built anything yet, she trusted in her ability to put things together – she'd always managed to figure it out when it came to jewellery, and that had to be a good start! As for Peter, Layla hadn't seen him around for a while (*maybe I've scared him off!*) and all her other classes were ticking along just fine (*Ms T seems to even kinda like me now!*). As for what was wrong with Ethan, well. Hmm, that might need some further investigating!

When Layla arrived at the pick-up area, she was puffed. Her scarf had slipped backwards, and a bunch of tight black afro curls had popped out and made an appearance. Beads of sweat ran down her face, and she wiped her forehead with her sleeve to soak up some of the perspiration, leaving a damp spot on her cream blouse.

Her family car was one of the handful in the pick-up area, and she could see her dad sitting in the front, eyes closed, hands on the steering wheel. Layla hoped he was listening to some Qur'an or something peaceful so she wouldn't get into any trouble!

Layla trotted up to the car and opened the rear door. The icy air of the air conditioning billowed out, almost instantly drying the sweat on her face. The sonorous voice of her father's favourite radio presenter droned out of the speakers, and Layla breathed a sigh of relief: Baba never got mad when he was listening to this radio show.

'Hey, Baba!' Layla squeaked chirpily, throwing her backpack on to the back seat before shutting the door and jumping into the front.

'*Mmmm*, Layla, *kayfik*?' Baba responded in Arabic, asking how her day was. He must have really been enjoying the radio, as he made no mention of her tardiness. They travelled all the way home without talking, just quietly listening to the delightful voice through the speakers. Layla leaned her head against the window and breathed deeply, closing her eyes, relaxed.

When she opened her eyes, she was surrounded by darkness. She felt her shoulder being shaken and realized her dad was trying to wake her up.

'*Yallah ya*, Layla. We're home!' She hadn't even realized she had fallen asleep, but her nap had lasted the whole trip home.

At dinner that night, her parents asked her how things were progressing.

'Good, *Alhamdulillah*!' she said, enthused at her progress. 'I know what the whole thing is going to look like. I've designed a body for the bear, got a plan for how I am going to make the gummy worm actuator arms, and now I just need to start building and testing!'

Her parents beamed at her, pleased. They were still unsure about whether this was a winning bet, but they were supportive of Layla. When she worked hard she could make almost anything happen.

'Mama, I'm going to need help with a few things. Can we go to the shops and find a mould that will work, and also start testing the gummy-worm melting mixture?'

Fadia nodded. 'Yes, we can go after dinner, *inshallah*. Oz, you can come too if you'd like to drop a few more résumés off?'

Ozzie bristled. 'I already did, Ma. I told you that. I've handed my résumé in to every single place in the shopping centre. No one has got back to me, even though some of them have signs out the front saying they are looking to hire people!'

Fadia frowned. 'Maybe I can ask around at the hospital to see if there are any entry-level jobs. I know you don't want me to help, but surely it's not a bad idea?'

Ozzie closed his eyes and muttered under his breath, 'OK, fine, whatever.'

Layla felt for her brother, but her mind was somewhere else. She was focused on getting what she needed for the Huggy Bear. Layla had known exactly where to go: her favourite store, Dollars and Cents. It was her domain. She'd spent years as a child running up and down the overcrowded aisles while her father was shopping for the week's groceries. D&C had all kinds of strange items: super cheap confectionery (Layla knew they were in aisle eight just behind the wrapping paper section), arts and crafts materials (that's where she sourced all her good beads and string from), random electronics, stationery, furniture, souvenirs, cooking utensils. Whatever you could dream up, D&C had it. But today, she wasn't there for the jewellery section. No, today she was there because she wanted to make something different. In her late-night shopping outfit of black skinny jeans, red Converse shoes and an oversized hoodie, Layla strode into the store, picked up a basket and skipped into aisle eight, where she knew the sweets would be.

Let's get to it! And they shopped for gummy actuator parts like there was no tomorrow.

Back home, Layla stood at the stove, slowly adding gummy worms to a saucepan of boiling water. Baba was standing next to her, offering advice and instructions.

'Now, I don't know much about robots,' Kareem said. 'But if we're doing some cooking, I've got you covered.' Baba loved to cook, and his culinary skills were turning out to be unexpectedly useful for this competition.

Layla stood over the saucepan, slowly stirring the thick greeny-red goo that used to be three packets of delicious gummy worms. Bubbles slowly and lazily pushed their way to the surface as the goo simmered over the heat. It was thick like honey, and it smelled like gummy worms tasted – delicious. Layla breathed in deeply, the steam warming her nostrils and dampening her face.

'All right, that looks like it's about the right consistency,' Baba said after about half an hour of slow stirring. 'Let's put it in the mould.'

Layla nodded and grabbed a tea towel from the rack to insulate herself from the saucepan heat. Wrapping the grey furry towel round the handle, she lifted the saucepan, with the goo still simmering, then put it on a place mat on top of the marble benchtop. She started to ladle the goo into one of the D&C moulds – a cheap white plastic. The goo trickled slowly from the spoon, and Layla wiggled the utensil slightly to speed it up.

'*La, la,*' Baba interrupted her when he noticed Layla's movement. 'Don't try to make it go any faster because you don't want to create air bubbles in the mould, *habibti*. Just let it settle in naturally.'

Layla nodded and waited. Once all five moulds were filled, she placed them in a cool corner on the kitchen bench, cleaned up the kitchen and went to bed. Tomorrow was Friday, and she would hope-fully be able to test the actuators at school. If they worked, she was in business for the competition next week. If it didn't work . . . well, she couldn't really think about that now, could she?

As she drifted off to sleep, her quilt up to her chin, Layla's mind started to wander. It was in quiet moments like this that she would usually begin to stress herself out. She wondered about the other competitors for the first time. What was Peter's group making? What would the other schools be like? Had she forgotten anything? A knot started to form in her stomach, and her mind raced.

Was she good enough? She'd always won competitions where you had to make things, but that was at ISB. This was different, these were people with a lot of money, a lot of support, and they all had big teams – she was all by herself! What had she done?!

Layla squeezed her eyes closed tightly, and willed her mind to stop.

Breathe, she reminded herself. *Breathe!*

Then she started the one thing that always helped clear her mind just before she went to sleep. She started *tasbee7*. Sometimes Layla used a string of beads to keep count, sometimes she just counted on her fingers. Tonight, Layla was all about the fingers. Three touches of each digit beginning with her index finger on her thumb, and then switching so her thumb touched the top, middle and bottom of every other finger. Layla repeated the ritual three times in a row, making it forty-five in total. *Subhanallah*, forty-five times; *Alhamdulillah*, forty-five times; *Allah-hu-Akbar*, forty-five times.

It was a ritual that she had seen her mother often do after praying, but it had been one night in Sudan as a little girl, when she couldn't sleep, that Grandma had suggested she do the same. It was a kind of Muslim meditation, and almost always worked wonders.

Chapter 18

The next morning before class, moulds in hand, Layla strode into the tech room looking for Mr Gilvarry.

'Mr G! Mr G!' she yelled, walking through the workshop and into the adjoining rooms. She heard muffled voices from behind a closed door – a room she had never been into. It was the senior school workshop, and it had the *big* machines. Layla was a little intimidated by them, if she was honest. But today she could hear Mr Gilvarry's booming voice coming from the other side of that door, so there was no time to waste.

Layla placed her hand round the door handle, the smooth metal surface cool to the touch. The door was made of reinforced steel, with large rivets on its inside edge, reminiscent of a bank vault. It was much heavier than she expected it to be. Layla resorted to using her body weight, leaning her shoulder against the door to push it open. The movement caused a scandalously loud screech on the concrete floor, so everyone in the room turned round at once. Door fully open, Layla stood in the entrance, embarrassed.

In the room was Mr Gilvarry, Peter and four other members of his team, all crowded round a large robot in the centre of the main workshop table. Gilvarry was in his usual bus-driver get-up, but he also had on a large dark red PVC apron, making him look like a terrifying *MasterChef* competitor, if the TV show was for cooking up robots rather than food. Peter and the rest of the boys were in dark blue work overalls with lots of pockets and reflective safety strips across their bellies and arms. Layla recognized only Matty from her class; the other boys all looked older.

Peter clocked Layla as she walked in, and his face twisted in recognition before he dismissively turned away from her and back to the robot in front of him.

The robot on the desk was, in one word, *magnificent*. The boys had clearly been working on it for some time – it was humanoid-looking, the size of a small child, with an iPad screen instead of a head. The body and legs of the robot were held up by a neat skeleton of Meccano pieces, draped in 'skin' made from what appeared to be an opaque carbon fibre the colour of toffee. Instead of feet, there were wheels: thick, fat wheels with deep treads, clearly enabling it to traverse all sorts of terrain. But the arms of the robot looked unfinished – the skeleton was there, joined to the body at the shoulders, but there were no hands. And it looked like Layla had interrupted a debate about the hands: a few different prototypes littered the table around the robot, and Peter picked one up to fiddle with it.

Gilvarry looked at her. 'Ah, Layla! Good to see you. These boys are just working out a final kink in their project – how are you going with yours?'

Layla realized she was holding the moulds in her hand and quickly hid them behind her back.

'Oh, yeh, good,' she replied uncertainly.

Seeing Peter's robot had made her feel incredibly self-conscious about her edible robot. How could something she came up with in one night beat something like . . . whatever *that* was? *Well, at least I don't have to deal with a huge team!* She had the benefit of being able to make all the decisions, and then take all of the credit! YASSS!

Layla focused on her teacher. 'Actually, I was wondering if I could get your help doing a test?'

Gilvarry's moustache bristled in what Layla assumed was a movement of approval. He turned to look back at Peter's team, who had resumed a quiet discussion about one of the prototype hands. 'You boys all right here?' Gilvarry asked.

Matty looked up and nodded.

Gilvarry dusted his hands on his apron and walked towards Layla. 'All right then, lass. Let's have a look at what we can do.'

Gilvarry closed the door behind them, lifting it slightly from the ground so it wouldn't cause a mind-bending screech. He winked at Layla. 'This building has all sorts of little idiosyncrasies, lass. It's all about getting to know how something works and making it work for you.'

Layla nodded, and followed Gilvarry into the junior students' workshop, where she felt quite comfortable – particularly compared to the big kids' workshop. Gilvarry stood in the middle of the room, and Layla continued past him towards the workbench closest to the air hose.

'OK, I have these moulds, and I want to see if they can be actuated.' Layla placed the moulds she had been hiding behind her back on the table. They looked so small compared to that huge humanoid thing Peter's team had built. Huggy Bear seemed so lame now . . .

Gilvarry clasped his calloused hands behind his back and he leaned down to look at the multicoloured moulds. His red beard tickled the surface of the workbench as he scrutinized Layla's work. 'Hmmmm, interesting!' he muttered under his breath, moustache twitching. 'So these are edible, are they?' Unclasping his hands from behind his back, he placed his left hand in his pocket and picked up a mould with his right, squeezing it between his index finger and thumb. Gilvarry's hands were large and hairy, and the mould looked like a tiny toy between his sausage-like fingers. He brought it closer to his face, squinting as he inspected it. Then, in one swift movement, he opened his mouth, threw the mould in and started chewing.

'Sir!' Layla yelled, shocked. What was he doing? They were supposed to be testing whether the moulds worked with the air hose, not eating them! This wasn't part of the plan! She had only brought five pieces anyway, and now she was down to four.

'Oh well, you said you wanted to test the pieces, didn't you? And they're supposed to be edible actuators? I'm just testing if they're edible first!' Gilvarry said, beaming at Layla's incredulous expression. Gilvarry smacked his lips together. 'And you know, I must say, they *are* quite delicious!' he said, chortling, his belly rolling with laughter. Slapping his stomach with both hands and then rubbing them together, Gilvarry quickly became serious. 'That being said though, lassie, we do need to test if these delicious blocks actually do actuate, don't we?'

Layla nodded. That *was* why she was here, after all – not to have her hard work eaten up by her teacher!

'And you said these would be air-actuated?'

Layla nodded again.

'All right, then, let's see how we go.'

Gilvarry walked over to the air hose and switched on the diesel engine linked to the pneumatic pump. He brought the hose over to the workbench, fixed on a nozzle that would fit the gummy worm arms and then attached the nozzle, ready for testing.

'All right, Layla,' Gilvarry said in his deep and serious workshop voice. 'Head over to the air hose over there and read out the pressure reading on the gauge. We might have to test a few different pressures to make this work. Once you've checked the pressure reading, press the big green button labelled "AIR", and the correct amount of pressure will come down through the hose and into this little worm you've got here.'

Layla nodded again, slowly walking over to the coiled air hose and pump set-up. The pump itself was sitting underneath the coiled hose. Layla crouched down so she was at eye level, and ran her hand over the top surface, eyes scanning for the gauge and button. The pump was covered in a thin layer of dust and oil – it looked like it hadn't been used in a long, long time. Layla gulped, hoping this would work.

Layla found the gauge tucked at the back between the concrete wall of the room and the pump. Using her thumb to wipe the scum off the front face, she squinted, trying to make sense of the faint markings on the gauge's face.

'Sir, there are two sets of numbers here?' she yelled out to Gilvarry.

'Ah yes! Good work, Layla. The inside numbers are *bars* and they're related to atmospheric pressure. It's probably not going to be useful for us. Read the outside numbers, which should be in black – those are in PSI, or pounds per square inch.'

'Ah, all right,' Layla replied uncertainly. 'I think we're at about eighty PSI?'

'Good work. All right. Let me just get my gloves on and we will test this little gal out, shall we?'

Gilvarry pulled out a set of tough-looking grey leather gloves from the front pocket of his apron and quickly donned them. Then, with a nimbleness that seemed impossible given how thick the gloves looked, he picked up the small gummy worm mould attached to the air hose, and then glanced at Layla, who was still crouched beside the pump. Her cream shirt had grease marks on the front, and her long skirt ballooned around her, giving her the appearance of a brown fairy on a maroon lily pad.

Gilvarry nodded at Layla. 'All right, lassie. Switch it on!'

Layla breathed in, then pressed the green button right next to the gauge. She pressed down once, hard, then let go. The pump made a strange sound – *thud*, *thud*, *thud*, *thud* – and Layla was worried that she'd broken something, but Gilvarry looked unperturbed.

'That's the sound it's supposed to make. Now . . .'

As he talked, the gummy worm mould started to move! The mould, which was straight and about the size of Gilvarry's finger, began to curve. Slowly at first, and then faster and faster, until it began to coil in on itself and stretch longer, and then . . . *BANG!*

The gummy arm exploded, bits of red and green gummy worm flying all over the room and right into Mr Gilvarry's face. The teacher's beard was covered in specks, and a chunk hung off the edge of his moustache. Gilvarry looked down, poked his tongue out and licked it off his bristly facial hair.

Layla had jumped up at the noise, tripping slightly on her skirt.

'Ha!' he chortled. 'Well, clearly eighty PSI is a little too much! Let's try that again with another worm. Hopefully we have enough to get it right, hmm?'

They tried 50 PSI and 25 PSI, and both of those moulds exploded in a similar fashion, though not as loudly. With the final one, Gilvarry suggested they try with a much, much smaller number.

'Let's go the other way, shall we? Try putting it in 1 PSI, and we will slowly increase the pressure to see what works.'

One PSI, the arm barely moved. Two, and there was a slight twitch. Three PSI and the arm curved and then . . . stopped! Just at the point where the mould looked like a bent finger.

'Oh, it worked!' Layla clapped her hands, excited. She had been holding her breath nervously, as not only was this the last mould she had brought, but it was really hard to read the gauge accurately on such a small face. But, it had worked! *Alhamdulillah!*

'Well done!' Mr Gilvarry said approvingly. 'It looks like you're all set! You'll just whack these arms on whatever body design you've got, and you're good to go.' Gilvarry ran his sausage fingers through his beard. 'Have you thought about whether there is another way to get enough air into these arms?' Layla shook her head. 'If this is going to be big, you might need to consider it, because these pneumatic pumps are a little expensive.' Gilvarry smiled. 'But let's not get ahead of ourselves. I emailed you all the instructions for the competition on Monday. Make sure you get in nice and early, so you can get a good spot to set up your demonstration.'

Layla nodded absentmindedly. All right, it was crunch time. Or perhaps she should call it candy crunch time. *Hehe. Hehe.*

★

That weekend, Layla spent the days threading liquorice cubes on to wooden skewers, making a bear shape out of the sweets. Dina came over on Saturday afternoon and helped – even though Layla was technically in Shutdown Mode, Dina knew the drill. Layla also totally avoided social media that weekend. *It's because of Shutdown Mode.* She told herself this pretty convincingly, but deep down she knew it was because she didn't want to see all the Snaps of Baz's huge party. Instead of focusing on her FOMO, Layla focused on building her creations with Dina. Together they built a whole family of Huggy Bears, like a Huggy Bear version of the Husseins. The twins loved their replica Huggys, posing excitedly for selfies with them on Sunday evening. Ozzie's replica even got a bit of candyfloss on top of his lollipop head as a cool afro, which he was clearly pleased about (although he'd never admit it).

The actuator arms were attached to the bodies using some clear fishing wire, which Layla had in her jewellery-making kit, threaded through the gummy worm arms and then tied to the wooden skewers in between the liquorice blocks. There was a little bit of slack in the wire too, to allow for the movement of the arms as they curved. Layla was pleased with the results and sang to herself as she packed the Huggy Bears into plastic containers, ready for transportation the next morning. As she laid each bear down into its clear shipping container she whispered a little *dua*.

'*Inshallah* this will all be worth it,' she muttered as a plea to Allah.

Dina smiled at her best friend as they cleaned up the kitchen table at the end of the day. 'You got this, gurl. Queen Laylz always wins.'

Layla smiled back and nodded, tired but determined. Into the fridge the Huggy Bears all went, and off to bed Layla traipsed. Tomorrow was a big day.

Chapter 19

Layla's sleep was dreamless. She woke up before her alarm, before Baba even walked into her room to shake her awake. The sun had yet to fully come up.

Ah! She could pray *fajr* on time today, blearily rubbing her eyes. Grunting, she got out of bed and slipped into her rubber slides. Layla walked to the bathroom and splashed water on her face before she did *wudhu*. Drying off, she shuffled back into her room and pulled her prayer scarf over her head – a large white scarf made from light material that covered her head and arms, all the way down to her knees. As she stood at the foot of the prayer mat facing Mecca, she felt a cool sense of calm wash over her.

Whatever happens today, Allah's got my back.

She raised her hands to her ears. *Allah-hu-Akbar!*

Layla's hands shook with nervousness as she got out of the car. They had arrived at the hall where the Grand Designs Tourismo was being held. The hall was in the middle of the city, and usually held large concerts and exhibitions. Layla had been to some of those exhibitions before – a big secondhand book sale, a jewellery-making exhibition. She'd even been pulled along to one on houses (that was more Mama's interest). But Layla had never expected that one day she would be exhibiting something here *herself.*

After parking the car deep underground, Baba helped her carry her lunchbox shipping containers into the lift. When the lift doors opened, Layla gasped sharply. The enormous hallway, usually large enough to play a football match in, was *packed.* There were parents and teachers, students walking around in teams holding all sorts of boxes and contraptions, kids running around, even a news camera crew near one of the doors. On the other side of the hallway from the lift, Layla spied a large banner with the word REGISTRATION. She pointed to the sign and motioned for her father to follow.

As they stood in the registration line, something started to gnaw at Layla. The people in front of her all had a packet of something in their hands, and they each had an A5-shaped landscape placard pinned to the front of their shirts with a large number.

Why don't I have one of those?

As she looked around, she realized all the students had a similar placard. A bead of sweat started to form on Layla's temple.

Baba, who had been enjoying himself by looking around at the melee, noticed Layla's unusual silence.

'Everything OK? Don't worry about the size of the hall and the number of competitors. You've got a great project, *habibti*.'

Layla shook her head. 'No, it's not that, Baba. I think there might be another problem.'

Layla thought back to that conversation with Mr Gilvarry where she had tuned out. He had been talking about some sort of paperwork, right? At the time, she'd completely dismissed him, having gone into Shutdown Mode. But now, she wondered if she should have been listening.

They got to the front of the queue and were called up by one of the workers behind the registration desk. The desk was long and thin, with about ten people sitting behind the bench at intervals, all with name cards and paperwork in front of them. The lady who called Layla up had black voluminous curls, quirky-shaped red glasses and freckles on her deep brown skin. Layla walked over, oddly relieved she'd got the only brown-skinned person at the registration desk.

'What's your name and school, lovely?' the woman asked, her name tag indicating her name was Ms Taringa.

'I'm Layla Kareem Abdel-Hafiz Hussein,' she said, 'or just Layla Hussein for short, and I'm from MMGS.'

'Ah! Another student from Mary Maxmillion,' Ms Taringa said, smiling. 'Are you in any of the larger teams?'

'No, I'm here by myself, in a team of one,' Layla rasped proudly, despite the sick feeling in her stomach starting to creep up her throat.

'Hmm.' Ms Taringa's well-manicured eyebrows knitted together as she ran her thin pencil down the line of names on the paper in front of her. 'Hmm . . .' she made a tsking sound, got to the bottom of the page, flipped the paper over, and searched the names there as well. When she clearly hadn't found anything, she started again. 'Maybe it's under Layla and not Hussein . . .' she murmured quietly, almost to herself.

After a few minutes, Layla's throat was starting to close up with the stress. The registration lady glanced up at her with a puzzled look on her face. 'Did you submit all the paperwork in time, Layla?' she asked. 'I can't seem to find your name here at all, not under your first or last name, not even under a different school.'

Layla shook her head, wordless. She hadn't submitted any paperwork at all, but she didn't want to admit that just yet. This couldn't be happening. 'I'm not sure . . . I mean, my school has known about this for weeks – maybe ask Mr Gilvarry, the teacher in charge of all the teams?'

Ms Taringa smiled at the mention of the tech teacher. 'Ah! Mr Gilvarry! No worries. I will check with Mr Gilvarry. Is there anything you will need for your set-up? A power point, an air source, anything like that?'

Layla nodded. 'Yes, ma'am,' she said, her nervousness making her more formal. 'I'll need a pneumatic pump or air source near me.'

'All right.' Ms Taringa looked under a pile of papers in front of her and pulled up a map of the exhibition hall, which clearly marked areas with electricity sources, water sources and air sources.

'OK, air sources. You will be at the back of the hall. Here's a table number – go inside and start to set up.'

Ms Taringa handed Layla a small plastic card with the number 895 in bold letters.

Layla let out her breath in a quiet hiss. OK, maybe she would be able to get away with this.

'Layla, did you do the paperwork?' Baba asked, voice soft as they walked away from the registration desk.

Layla shook her head. She didn't want to talk.

'Let's just try to get through the first round, OK?' she whispered under her breath, shutting the conversation down.

The pair threaded through the crowd of people to make it to the front of the main exhibition hall. A tall, bald security guard in all black blocked the door, and when Layla approached he held out his beefy hand to stop her.

'Card,' he demanded, his voice dull with boredom.

Layla reached into her jacket pocket and fumbled for the plastic card she had just been given, handing it to the bouncer. He looked at the card, turned it over, flicked it and then handed it back, nodding.

'Good luck,' he said, equally tonelessly, then he stepped to one side to let them access the door.

Layla handed her father the boxes she was holding, pressed the bar on the door down and pushed both double doors open. The sight that they revealed was both glorious and intimidating.

Rather than the wild chaos that filled the hallway, the exhibition hall was cloaked in a library-like hush.

The ceiling was impossibly high, with bright fluorescent lights dropping down from the roof, illuminating the enormous room in a soft blue-white hue. Rows upon rows of tables stretched out in front of them, with groups of students in blazers of all colours and crests huddled round each table, whispering quietly. Other students were walking around, their movements fast and focused, reminding Layla of the way ants move in a determined, choreographed manner. The sight was truly awesome.

Layla looked up at her father, her face a mix of worry and excitement, the anxiety of registration forgotten. She'd never been to anything like this before. Gosh, this was exactly the reason why she'd wanted to attend MMGS – for things like this. Whatever happened, this was why she was at MMGS. This was *real* adventure.

Baba placed his hand on her shoulder and squeezed it reassuringly. '*Yallah, habibti*. Let's find your table.'

Layla and Baba weaved in and out of the tables, making their way towards the back of the room. They passed all sorts of contraptions and inventions:

walking plants, drones of different shapes and sizes, even a lamp that seemed to be able to talk. When they reached the back, they found Layla's desk and began to set up. A piece of paper with the judging schedule was sitting on the desk and Layla picked it up to read. 'OK, first round starts soon!'

'Do we need to go anywhere for it?' Baba asked, arranging the Huggy Bears on the table. The large surface of the table looked empty, with only the Huggy Bears to fill the space.

Layla looked around – it seemed other teams had brought props and signs to fill the space. She sighed. Wow, there was so much she was unprepared for. 'No, the judges come to us.'

'Ah, *khalas*. I guess we just sit and wait then?' Layla nodded in response. Before she sat down, she found the air source and tested the operation of the edible actuator arms. Fortunately, this pump had a digital read out, so she could pump exactly 3 PSI. As planned, the Huggy Bears all moved their arms in a hugging motion. They worked!

Now, just to wait.

Chapter 20

Layla had sat down for barely a moment before she saw a familiar red-bearded man making his way to her table.

'Mr Gilvarry!' she exclaimed happily, jumping out of her seat.

She was so excited to show her tech teacher what her final product looked like, but as soon as she saw his facial expression Layla was stopped in her tracks. Gilvarry wore a look of frustration, made even more obvious by the smooth, expressionless faces that flanked him. Her tech teacher had arrived with a man and woman in tow, tall, gangly and serious, and by the look of their suits, they were important.

When the three adults reached Layla's table, Gilvarry began to talk. Layla had never heard him sound so serious. His voice had lost every bit of its usual jovial quality.

'Layla, these two people are part of the Grand Designs Tourismo administration and they've come to me because there's no record of you having registered for the competition. If you haven't registered, Layla, you won't be able to compete.' Mr Gilvarry's face was so red that his skin colour matched his beard and moustache.

Layla couldn't tell if he was angry at her or the admin people. 'I reminded you to register a little while back, do you remember? You did register, yes? Show them your paperwork.'

Layla's stomach dropped past her feet and into the ground. It fell so far it pretty much hit magma. She swallowed, her mouth suddenly very dry. 'Oh . . .'

Her throat closed up, and no more words came out. Layla started fiddling with the edge of her scarf. How was she going to tell these people that she had made such a big mistake – another huge mistake? She was definitely going to get kicked out of MMGS now!

Baba, who had been standing to the side listening, stepped up to the table. 'I'm sorry, but it would appear that my daughter hasn't actually completed the paperwork required. Is there a way she can participate anyway? We've worked very hard on the project, and it's quite a novel invention: edible actuators!'

For the first time since they'd arrived, both administrators' faces betrayed signs of emotion.

'That does sound quite interesting,' one administrator said, exchanging a glance with the other.

Layla's heart skipped a beat – were they impressed enough by her idea that they would let her compete?

Apparently not. The second administrator shook his head. 'That may be so,' he said, 'but if you haven't registered a team, you can't compete. The only option is for you to join another team from MMGS and somehow combine your projects.'

The woman nodded, consulting her clipboard. 'Yes. It looks like the other teams from your school have the maximum number of members except for –' her fingernail traced down the list on the page – 'except for Mr Peter Cox's team.'

'You have until the beginning of round two of the judging to make your decision. You either join Mr Cox's team, or you forfeit your chance to compete at the GDT,' said the other administrator tightly.

With that proclamation, both administrators spun on their heels and walked away, leaving Mr Gilvarry standing in front of Layla and her father. All three of them stood in stunned silence.

'*Ya-nhar-aswad*, no, no, no, no . . .' Layla's voice broke, and tears started streaming down her face. *No!* How could this have happened? How could it have come down to this? How did she miss something so obvious as MAKING SURE SHE HAD REGISTERED?!

Layla's mind felt like scrambled eggs, and she thought she was going to vomit. This was it. This was the end of the line. Slowly, Layla's legs gave way, and she sank to the floor, burying her face in the skirt material covering her knees. She took a deep, shuddering breath in, and then let out a high-pitched wail. It sounded like the whine of a motor warming up, so nobody in the room even blinked at the sound.

'Layla!' Baba crouched down next to her and started rubbing her back comfortingly. 'It's OK, *habibti*. We will figure this out.'

Standing back up, her father addressed the tech teacher standing in front of him, hands in pockets. Gilvarry looked down at the table. 'I don't know what to say,' Baba said to him, and Gilvarry shrugged his shoulders.

'Aye, I did say to the lass that she needed to register, but I should have checked. She'll have to join the Cox boy's group.' Gilvarry pointed to a table a few rows down, where the maroon blazers of MMGS were visible. 'Otherwise, you're both going to have to pack up and leave. That's simply how it is. I'm really sorry, because I really love your daughter's work, sir, but this one is out of my hands.' Gilvarry scratched the back of his head and shrugged, then walked away, bus-driver socks and all.

Layla was still down on the floor, crouching and refusing to acknowledge what was going on around her.

'All right, let's go outside and get some fresh air,' her father suggested, and she looked up at him, sniffling, and nodded. Baba handed her his pocket handkerchief, a grey cotton square he always kept neatly folded in his trousers. 'Wipe your face, blow your nose and let's go.'

They found a bench across the road from the exhibition hall. Baba bought them an ice cream each from the nearby shop, and so they sat side by side, father and daughter, eating their cones in silence.

Once Baba finished his cone, he folded the cardboard packaging it had come in and threw it in the bin next to the bench. He then turned to Layla.

'OK. You're going to need to figure out a way through this. You made a mistake by not checking what the registration process was when you got involved in this project, right?'

Layla nodded. She was going to have to accept that she wasn't great with responsibility, especially because it seemed Mr Gilvarry had tried to remind her to register and she'd just tuned him out.

'But you have worked really hard on your idea.'

Layla nodded again. 'It's a bit silly now though, isn't it?'

Kareem tilted his head, considering. 'Not necessarily. I mean, there were lots of things throughout history that I am sure would have been weird when they were invented, but when you find the proper use for them, it seems very obvious that they are important items for our everyday lives. You don't quite know the value of what you have invented yet, but that doesn't mean it doesn't have value,' he said. 'But that's not the biggest problem. Your biggest problem right now is how you are going to be a part of this competition, and secure your future, without your own team.'

Layla dropped her head into her hands. This was a complete nightmare. She'd worked so hard to get into a school like MMGS, all on her own, and now she'd ruined that so quickly. She'd got suspended, she'd been rude to teachers, she'd invented something super weird and she couldn't even keep on top of the paperwork she needed to do. How had things got so out of hand?

She was so tired of feeling angry and exhausted. She just wanted it all worked out.

All of a sudden, a freckly face framed in red curls popped into her mind. Ah, Ethan . . . what would Ethan say in a moment like this? Layla wasn't sure if she knew Ethan well enough yet, but she had a feeling he would echo what so many people had said to her over the past few weeks. Find a way to make it work with the boy she hated. Peter Cox. Swallow her pride. Channel the *jamel*. Be a Queen.

Layla lifted her head out of her hands and looked at her father. 'I need to talk to Cox, don't I?' she said.

Her father shrugged. 'It might be your only chance,' he said, 'but I understand it will be difficult. Just focus on what's important to you. Is it winning the competition, or beating Peter? You might not be able to have both.'

Layla walked back into the hallway and bumped into Matty from Cox's group. He looked slightly frazzled and distracted, his hair sticking up at odd angles.

'Hey, Matty, how's it going?' Layla asked, hoping to get his help in finding a way to join the team.

Matty's eyes, which darted from left to right, finally focused on Layla in front of him.

'Oh, yeh, um, fine,' he muttered. 'Yeh.' He swallowed. 'Good, good.'

He blinked, taking a deep breath in and then rubbing his hands down the front of his jacket, smoothing it down. 'Yeh, it's all going good. The robot is working, so we're excited. We find out if we made it through the first round pretty soon, but, I mean, ha! Of course we will!' Matty laughed awkwardly.

Layla nodded. 'So, what is it that your robot actually does?' she asked, curious. She'd seen the thing move around on the table on those wheels, but the iPad face was a bit weird.

'Oh, it's like a portable telepresence robot – so it can help kids who can't get to school learn via the robot – it cruises round classes, and you can FaceTime with the iPad screen. It's also good for, like, old people. It can help them around the house and stuff . . .' Matty's voice trailed off and his eyes focused on something behind

Layla. 'Hey, sorry, I've gotta run,' he said, abruptly pushing past Layla and sprinting into the exhibition hall.

Hmm, that was a bit strange, wasn't it? Matty was very distracted. Layla's eyes widened as she remembered the scene from the senior students' tech room she'd walked into last week. They were playing with robotic hands and it had looked like they were having a big discussion! And Matty hadn't mentioned hands at all. Maybe there was something there . . .

Layla started running too. She looked at the large digital screen on the wall above the doors, which had the schedule for the day. The first round was now complete and the second round started in half an hour. If she was to join Cox's team, she needed to convince him to let her help in the next thirty minutes! *Bismillah!*

She spotted the group's table across the hall and ran over. As she got closer, she could hear them having an argument.

OK, go in gently, she told herself.

Slowing down, she walked over to the table. Peter looked up and spotted her, his mouth twisting venomously.

'What do you want?' he snarled at her.

Layla's heart skipped a beat. She just wanted to punch this guy! Who did he think he was, talking to her like that? But she couldn't, so she breathed in, deeply, and thought of Nelson Mandela. If he could work with people who hated him, she could too.

'Hey, Peter,' she said tentatively, approaching the table with confidence. Matty moved aside to let her in. 'So, here's the thing. I didn't actually register my team, so I can't compete.'

Peter chuckled disdainfully.

'But a little birdie told me that perhaps you could use my help. And since I don't want to go back to school today, I thought I'd offer my services rather than sit around and be bored.'

Peter laughed mockingly, but Layla could see that his eyes were also nervous. 'What on earth could you offer that we would need?' he asked. The rest of the group shuffled, uncomfortable with the dynamic.

'Well.' Layla hoped this punt was going to pay off. 'I heard you were having a few problems with your hands.' She looked pointedly at the ends of the telepresence robot's arms.

They were bare.

'Damn! Who told you?' Peter burst out, his voice clearly betraying his frustration and embarrassment.

Layla put her hands up reassuringly. She admitted the truth. 'No one told me, Peter. I figured it out on my own. Now, I think I can help you, but I have two conditions.'

Peter looked at her suspiciously. 'What conditions?'

'Well, firstly, I join the team. And I need to join the team before the second round, otherwise I'm disqualified.'

'If your plan fixes our hand problem, then you are part of the team,' Peter said, his voice cautious. 'What is the second condition?'

'I want you to admit what you did that first day at school and tell the principal and your dad.'

Layla felt the group around her stiffen. Clearly this was a big ask, but on her way here, Layla had figured that if she was going to bite her tongue and forgive, Peter should at least have to acknowledge what he'd done.

The bully stood in front of her, frozen. Layla studied his face. He looked like his mind was racing. She'd taken a big gamble with asking him to swallow his pride, especially in front of his team – she knew this wasn't the way that all the famous people in history worked. What was it that Ms T had said? Don't challenge someone's ego . . .

'And don't say they won't believe you. I've got video to show what you did.' Layla pulled out her phone and started playing the video that Leesa had sent her. Although Layla and Leesa didn't hang out much, they'd started seeing each other at the pick-up area after school, and soon became friends via Tumblr and Snapchat. When the young Syrian-Australian had realized the video she'd recorded could help Layla in some way, she'd sent a copy straight over. Layla hadn't wanted to resort to using this video (it felt a bit shady), but at the end of the day, this competition was her last chance to keep that scholarship and stay on the path to her dreams. Queens do what they need to do, and, sometimes, their hands get a little dirty. *Ya Allah, forgive me!* Layla prayed silently.

The entire group craned their necks to watch the video on Layla's phone, and collectively gasped as the image of Peter pushing Layla over and over again until she fell to the ground played out in front of them. Peter wasn't watching the video, though; he was staring right at Layla, who was staring right back. She saw something strange flicker behind his pupils, like the young man was troubled. That couldn't be possible. Peter was the bully here. Right?

As the video ended, he finally spoke. 'Fine, I did it. You can join.' His voice was short, clipped. But there it was.

Wow, that was quick. So much easier than Layla had expected. *I wonder why . . .*

Layla held his gaze. 'Thank you. But I have one more thing. Can you apologize to me now? Here . . . so we can both forgive each other and move on?' Layla spread her arms wide, motioning to everyone standing around them, watching closely.

Peter scrunched up his face, scowling. 'Get out of here. That wasn't one of the conditions! Plus, you owe me an apology! I had a bruise for weeks!'

Layla had seen how quickly he'd acquiesced to her conditions and realized this project was just as important to him as it was to her. And now that she had the floor, she was going to set the record straight.

'Peter, you're right. That wasn't one of the conditions, so you don't have to apologize now. But you need to understand how hurtful your comments are, and how hard you have made life for me.' Layla straightened her spine, threw her shoulders back and channelled her inner Queen. 'You should know that your actions hurt others, in the same way that other people hurt you. I'm sorry for being mean to you, headbutting you and calling you names. It's not cool. But that goes for both of us. I dunno what's going on with you, but we can't just spray our pain on everyone else. So, here's a chance to set it right.'

Matty and the other boys were all staring at Layla during this monologue, then they turned to look at Peter. It was like a tennis match, the ball the elephant in the room.

Peter was looking down at the table, his hands balled into fists, knuckles down on the desk. A muscle twitched in his jaw. The tension was as thick as gummy goo.

Layla was just about to say something when Peter lifted his head and looked Layla straight in the eyes.

'Look. I dunno what voodoo stuff you've got going on, and how you're getting into my head. But fine. I've got my own stuff going on, OK? My dad goes on and on and on about the GDT, how it's the best competition in the world and how the Coxes are destined to win it. Do you know what that pressure is like?' Peter's voice cracked. 'After my brother's team failed, I just have to win, OK. I just have to. And you come up in here with your huge skirt and loud laugh and wild headscarf and are all, "Look at me, I'm Layla!" and you think you're the best? And then you want to be in this competition and take it all from me? Do you know how much my dad would hate me if that happened? Do you know how hard I've had to fight for him to even notice me? God, it makes me hate you.' Peter swallowed, his Adam's apple bobbing up and down. 'But I know it's not really about you. Whatever, OK? Fine. My bad. SORRY.'

Layla stood in front of Peter, slightly stunned by the boy's confession. The monologue rang out loud and clear in the large, quiet hall. Layla almost felt for Peter. Who knew that he was under so much pressure? Ethan was right. Everyone really is fighting their own battles. *Janey Mack*, this was so intense.

'But that's enough mushy stuff. Let's get this damn thing fixed ASAP!' Turning round, Peter punched the desk, his words like jabs in the air, ending the emotional conversation. It was all robot from here.

Layla smiled to herself. For a moment, Peter was a different person. And although his yelling and aggressive manner were right back, that moment of humanity had given her something to work with. In so many ways, he really was just like everyone else.

Maybe being kind did have its perks!

It turned out that the problem was quite simple: they wanted to use robot hands or fingers as grippers that would pick up sensitive items, like eggs, without crushing them. The ones they were trialling were made out of metal or silicone, but they were all using too much force, so would crush the delicate items they tried to pick up in the demonstration.

'What PSI are you using for the silicone hands?' Layla asked.

'Like, twenty-five?' was Matty's response, who was in charge of the air-hose operation. 'They don't work at any lower PSI.'

Layla smiled and fished the Huggy Bear arms from her pockets. She had thought these might come in handy.

'How about trying these? I made them for my project, but since I can't use them, perhaps we can attach them on to your robot.'

'What are those? They look gross as!' Peter's face, always full of expression, looked slightly revolted.

'They're gummy worms all melted together to make edible actuators!' Layla said proudly. 'And they work at about three PSI! Perfect for lifting an egg, yeh?'

By combining forces, the team made it to the final round of the competition, eventually winning second place. That meant they would progress to the national finals in Sydney. When the awards were presented for first, second and third place at the end of the day, Layla stood proudly on stage next to Peter, laughing quietly to herself, enormously relieved. Mr Gilvarry sat next to her father in the front row of the audience, beaming up at them both through his bushy beard.

Alhamdulillah. She had made it to the national competition. She had proven that she belonged. She had made amends – kind of – with the boy who had caused her so much pain, and now, well, they were working together! They weren't the happiest family, but they were now family. *Speaking of family, where is Chairman Cox?* Layla couldn't see him in the crowd and wondered how Peter felt about his father's apparent absence. *Hmmm, he didn't even come to see the robot Peter made . . .*

Layla's train of thought was interrupted by her father waving from the crowd, motioning for her to smile as he took photos on his phone.

Wow. Almost everything had worked out.

Alhamdulillah.

Definitely not the way she'd expected, but wasn't that what life was about?

Chapter 21

That night at dinner, Layla recounted the drama of the day to her family.

Baba helped by adding bits and pieces to the story. He also shared how they had bumped into Peter's father, the chairman. It was just after the awards ceremony, when all the family members were gathering round the students.

'Mr Cox!' Kareem had said, with a strong handshake. 'It seems my daughter saved the day for your team!'

The tall, broad man looked at Peter, confused. Peter, resigned to the circumstances, relayed the story. 'Yeh, Dad. We wouldn't have got past the second round if it hadn't been for Layla's invention. And we probably can't go to nationals without her either.' Peter rolled his eyes, not totally excited by the situation. 'I know it's a drag, Dad, and I'm not joining any Layla fan clubs, but she is pretty good at what she does. She deserves the scholarship.' Peter looked over at Layla standing next to him with a strange glint in his eyes. 'And I guess I shouldn't be so mean to you. Cos it never feels nice when someone tries to put you down.'

Layla nodded sagely but didn't reply.

'And, well –' Peter cleared his throat and looked at the ground – 'I did push her on that first day of school, so, like, it wasn't totally all her fault . . .'

Layla's eyes widened as she turned her head and met her father's gaze. *Whoa, no way! He actually admitted it! WIN! Zero to Peter, One to the Queen.* Kareem's face barely changed, but Layla could see his moustache bristle, the telltale movement of her father hiding a smile. *OK, does that mean I can stay at the school?* Layla glanced up at the chairman hopefully.

Chairman Cox furrowed his brow, looking at his son reproachingly, then turned to Kareem. 'Well then,

I suppose there's more to the story than meets the eye. I'll have to discuss the probation with the principal next week. It appears young Layla has more to her than I first thought, and she certainly seems to have found a way to earn her place here, despite all the obstacles.

'As for you.' The man looked at his son with hands loosely clasped in front of him and a silver medal round his neck. Peter met his father's eyes, searching for a sliver of approval. 'Second place gets you to nationals. Make sure you win it next time.'

The words were cold, and despite Layla's glee at being given another chance, she felt the chill of the man's tone in her bones. Peter turned to leave, but Layla gripped his upper arm. He shrugged, trying to get her off, trying to leave the conversation, put distance between himself and his dad, but Layla wouldn't let him.

'Hey, Peter, hey!'

'What do you want?' he snarled, a snarl that Layla had always thought was due to his own cruelty, but was clearly just his way of hiding his fears and insecurities.

'You did a great job today,' she said to him. 'And your idea was lit. Don't worry about your dad.'

Peter looked at her, hard. His face was expressionless, his lips white. He shook his head. 'You don't get it. Your family came here to cheer you on, and they will always support you. My world is different. You don't realize that yours is a kind of privilege I will never feel.' With his other hand, he prised Layla's fingers from his arm and walked away through the throng of people milling about in the hall. Just before he disappeared out of sight though, he turned round and met Layla's eyes again, shrugging his shoulders. 'Thanks though,' he mouthed, then ducked his head and melded into the crowd.

As Layla finished the story at the dinner table, Ozzie shook his head.

'What's that about?' his mother asked him.

'Layla, I'm happy for you and everything, really I am. Good job on getting to work with that team, and for doing what you need to do to stay at that school. But I can't fully forgive guys like Peter. I just can't,' he said.

'Why?' Layla asked. She knew Ozzie had different experiences of the world, but this seemed pretty extreme, even for him.

'Because, at the end of the day, guys like him, even if they don't get love from their dads, they can still get a job. They can still afford nice cars and nice houses and won't get yelled at in the street. I can't even get a part-time job in a cafe. So I'm sorry for Peter that he fights with his dad, but that is *no* excuse, not in my book.'

It gave Layla food for thought. Maybe he was right.

The next day at school, things shone a little brighter. The team got their awards presented on stage, and Layla felt comfortable hanging with the crew at lunchtime. She wasn't friends with Peter as such, but they were on talking terms. The chat was all about the party that had happened on the weekend. She'd got away with not going because of the Grand Designs Tourismo, but her FOMO still sucked. It sucked a little less, though, because Ethan hadn't gone either. He didn't say why, so Layla figured something else was still going on.

On the way back from lunch, walking across the oval, Layla fell into step with Ethan. Her heart still fluttered every time she looked at his freckled face.

'Sorry, dude, I've been so distracted with the competition and all. How are you doing now? You were having a real hard time last week.'

Ethan gave Layla a sideways smile. 'Ha, yeh. I mean, I was a bit worried about something, because I haven't really told anyone else yet, but you seem cool. See, the thing is . . .'

Ethan stopped walking and pulled her aside. They were standing in the middle of the oval, but the space seemed to close in around them, like there was no one else in the world.

'I think I'm going to tell everyone else soon, but I wanted to tell you first.'

Layla's heart skipped. *This was the moment.*

'Layla, I'm gay. And I think I have a huge crush on Seb. I decided to come out to my parents last week. It wasn't the easiest, but we're OK now.'

A huge crush . . . on who?

Layla's eyes opened wide. 'Wait, what?'

Ethan's eyes also opened wide, and he looked panicked.

Layla then realized what her response had sounded like and quickly rearranged her face to show the happiness she felt for her friend, and the honour of being chosen to be confided in.

'Oh, Ethan! Thanks for sharing with me. I mean, to be honest, I'm kinda gutted cos I had a *huge* crush on you, but I guess that's really irrelevant now.'

Ethan laughed and then pulled her by her elbow towards the tech building. 'Yeh, I thought you might be getting a bit sweet on me, so that's why I thought I should tell you. I mean, gurl, if I was straight, I'd be all over ya, but I'm just as much into boys as you are! And I mean, c'mon, Seb is *super* cute, isn't he?'

Layla laughed loudly. 'OMG you are the worst. Seb is totally not my type. But I will tell you who else is . . .'

Lying in bed that night, with her phone on silent next to her head, Layla let the emotions of the last few weeks wash over her. Her quilt prickled on her bare arms, her braids pressed into the cotton of the pillow, rustling slightly. Cool air softly breezed in through the window, and the moon shone brightly on the prayer mat at the foot of her bed. Closing her eyes, she breathed in deeply.

What a time it had been!

She'd started at her dream school, although it wasn't quite what she'd imagined it would be. Yes, they had a workshop where she could build cool stuff and enter competitions that would take you around the world – everything that would help her be a fully fledged adventurer one day. But going to MMGS had been more complicated than she'd expected. She also couldn't really get away with nearly as much as she used to at ISB, and also . . . well, people were different. They didn't pray, they went to parties, they hung out in mixed groups. Layla had known she would stand out – *I mean, being the first* hijabi *at the school, I was definitely going to be different!* – but she hadn't realized how being different would make her *feel*.

I didn't think anyone's opinion really mattered to me, Layla conversed with herself, fingers playing with the end of her braid. *But I guess I do want people to like me.*

She wondered if that was a bad thing. Layla thought back to all the conversations she'd had about forgiving people, being kind, focusing on your own problems. She remembered how much she had enjoyed inventing something, solving an issue that might actually make a difference in people's lives. It wasn't quite bejewelling, but it definitely made her feel good.

Gosh, that was so satisfying! I wonder what else I can invent. I wonder what we will do for the national competition?! Thoughts of gummy-bear legs and animals began to pop into Layla's mind, though she quickly pushed them aside with a slight flick of her head. *No, no, enough gummy-bear thoughts for now. The next project has to be bigger and better . . .*

As Layla began to drift off to sleep, a final thought crossed her mind. Her mantra. Her eyes flicked open and she stared up in the darkness, the outline of the ceiling light made visible by the moonlight.

CHANNEL THE JAMEL!

Layla smiled to herself, thinking of her first day at MMGS. She'd walked in and Ms T had spotted her straight away.

'You must be Layla,' she'd said.

Layla hadn't understood why she had said that – or whether that was a good thing.

YAS, GURL. She closed her eyes again. *Yas. I am Layla. I'm loud, I'm weird, random, funny, smart. One day, I'm going to travel the world having adventures galore. I'm my own person . . . and I'll always be Layla. Don't you forget it.*

Glossary

3amalti shnu ya bit? – What did you do, girl?

3indi fikra – I have an idea

Aha yallah, guuli lehyna. Fikratik shinu? – OK, c'mon, tell us. What's your idea?

aha ya shabab – all right, everyone

Alhamdulillah – Thanks be to God (prayer)

al-jamel biyimshy, wa-al-kilab bitanba7 – the camel walks while the dogs keep barking

Allah-hu-Akbar – God is Great (prayer)

aywa – yes

baba – dad

barra7a – slowly

Bismillah – In the name of God (prayer)

cosa bi-al-bashamel – Sudanese dish

dua – to pray or perform an act of supplication

fajr – type of prayer

fi-al3asha – at dinnertime

habibi/habibti – darling

hijabi – girl or woman wearing a hijab

Inshallah – God willing

jalabeeya – a traditional Sudanese dress

kayfik? – How are you? (used for women)

khalas – all right then, or done

kisra – a traditional Sudanese dish

la – no

lisaan – tongue

Maghrib – fourth prayer of the day (just after sunset)

mama – mum

min ra3yatik – from your point of view

mufrak – wooden Sudanese cooking implement

mulaa7 – Sudanese dish

Rasoul – the Prophet

Salams – Peace

shakoosh – hammer

Subhanallah – God is perfect

shibshib – flip flops

tasbee7 – to pray, or act of supplication

tayyib – all right (Sudanese dialect)

toub – item of clothing

wudhu – the ritual washing before prayer

ya3ni – well, or kinda

ya bit – oh, girl

yallah – come on

ya-nhar-abyad! – Oh, white river! (Usually referring to the Nile, this is a phrase used like a curse word by grandmothers.)

ya-nhar-aswad! – Oh, black river!

About the Author

Yassmin Abdel-Magied is a Sudanese-born Australian writer, broadcaster and social advocate with a background in mechanical engineering.

Yassmin founded her first organization, Youth Without Borders, at the age of sixteen, published her debut memoir, *Yassmin's Story*, with Penguin Random House at age twenty-four, and followed up with her first fiction book for younger readers, *You Must Be Layla*, in 2019.

An advocate for the empowerment of women, youth and people of colour, Yassmin has been awarded numerous awards for her advocacy, including the 2018 Young Voltaire Award for Free Speech. Yassmin has travelled to over twenty countries speaking to governments, NGOs and multinational companies on a range of topics including unconscious bias, resilience, and the impact of technology on society. Her TED talk, 'What Does My Headscarf Mean to You?', has been viewed over two million times and was chosen as one of TED's top ten ideas of 2015. Yassmin's critically acclaimed essays have been published in numerous anthologies, including the *Griffith Review*, the bestselling *It's Not About the Burqa* and *The New Daughters of Africa*. Her words can also be found in publications like the *Guardian*, *Teen Vogue*, *The New York Times*, *The Independent* and *Glamour*.

Yassmin's broadcasting portfolio is diverse: she presented the national TV show *Australia Wide*, a podcast on becoming an F1 driver and created *Hijabistas*, a series looking at the modest fashion scene in Australia. Yassmin is a regular contributor to the BBC, Monocle 24 and is a co-host of *The Guilty Feminist*.

Outside advocacy, she worked as a drilling engineer on oil and gas rigs for four years and is an internationally accredited F1 journalist.

Introducing the bold new series,

EXTRAORDINARY LIVES

Packed full of incredible stories, fantastic facts and dynamic illustrations, EXTRAORDINARY LIVES shines a light on important modern and historical figures from all over the world.

Have you read about all of these extraordinary people?

THE EXTRAORDINARY LIFE OF
STEPHEN HAWKING

THE EXTRAORDINARY LIFE OF
MICHELLE OBAMA

THE EXTRAORDINARY LIFE OF
MALALA YOUSAFZAI

THE EXTRAORDINARY LIFE OF
ANNE FRANK

THE EXTRAORDINARY LIFE OF
KATHERINE JOHNSON

THE EXTRAORDINARY LIFE OF
NEIL ARMSTRONG

THE EXTRAORDINARY LIFE OF
MARY SEACOLE

THE EXTRAORDINARY LIFE OF
ROSA PARKS

THE EXTRAORDINARY LIFE OF
MAHATMA GANDHI